1

DELUGE OF SUSPICIONS

Marcus Sanford

Interplans.net
story development

DELUGE OF SUSPICION

Marcus Sanford, ask@interplans.net
November 2015
novels and scripts at Amazon.com

Contemporary crime fiction; history of science; cosmology; geology.

Special thanks to editorial and consulting readers: Jane Bultedaob, Patrick Nurre, Gerald Augberg, Daniel George

Contents

DELUGE OF SUSPICIONS

FOREWORD

In NATION OF SCARFACE, I attempted to rehearse a tribe leader that put together, or put back together, a moral code that actually made sense. If there was anything unrealistic about it, it was that it was more successful than most of them actually are.

This story is more realistic because a leading geologist who keeps all the orthodox points of uniformitarianism--but is far too isolated from a world that must make sense--is made to face the reality of where secular thinking goes. But more specifically, he has to realize that it generates race superiority which will eventually destroy the liberty that the Creator referenced in the American Constitution provided. He is damaged by what he believes—he can't make any distinctions. Yet he instinctively wants to. Will he figure out why? Or will he become a contradiction?

Unfortunately, he choses a contradictory life instead of a successful life. It's a tragedy and it is the direct result of evolutionary uniformitarianism. The upper class English intellectuals who put evolution together had no other way left to counter the American phenomenon than to write 'science' that undercut Biblical creation. While it attempted saved their class (they even took action to join and prevail with the Third Reich), it completely overlooked the most obvious things of geologic reality, and chose to ridicule the Biblical flood in various caricatures that are 'science at its worst.'

Instead of recognizing this, some students have simply denied that 'rights endowed by their Creator' is in the Constitution.

This story assembles the new catastrophic understanding of earth history and depicts the results of hardening one's self in the old versus opening one's self to the turbulent--and sometimes bizarre--world before the deluge.

Marcus Sanford
Fall 2015

Prologue

From beside the ancient Epeiric Sea...

A coastal warrior and his people's artist cautiously looked over the ocean. They talked about how they saw big land forms sink and rise at the ocean when they were young. They did not let their people live near the sea.

Everything had moved. The land, the oceans, even the stars were all changed. It was many years ago. They referred to the land forms as the 'lizard.' Some of them saw it move, buckle, foaming with waves. Some of them also saw 'god' walking there...they called him 'Vericocha' which means 'He Walks on the Foaming Waves.' They were not supposed to make pictures of him. But they could remember the foaming waves.

But now it was all settled.

They were now confident that Raven, who acted as creator, had finished off the 'lizard' since the land never moved any more, and the ocean had never been unsettled since then, only a little ways up and a little ways down. It was Raven who had flown out over all the raging oceans after the land collapsed and proved there was land again. It was Raven who was wise enough to build a 'raft' up high in a tree to survive another deluge if needed. They said he had shown a warrior and his families how to make a great raft during that deluge. That warrior took many animals with him in the raft and everyone now living came from him.

So now they were sure the land was not going to move, nor would the ocean charge around everywhere.

So the warrior instructed the artist to draw Raven killing the lizard. It was to be executed on a certain rock on the way from their village to the ocean. It was where their people could first see the ocean so that their people would know that the ocean was safe.

1

RELOCATIONS

The Snohomish River pulls together its several tributaries near Cathcart, Washington, within an hour from downtown Seattle. That's in smooth traffic. They include the Skykomish, the Tolt, the Sultan, and the Snoqualmie. Not included in the list is the Pilchuk. But during a storm it was the 'gathering' between Monroe and Cathcart that provided a knockout punch. At that point the Snoqualmie and the Skykomish joined and doubled the volume.

But this particular night, you could say it tripled, as the volume falling from above had to be somewhere close to contributing a third. Over at the local TV stations, the sterile term 'convergence zone' had been developed to name what happens here. Basically, weather from across the Pacific arrives here and gets stuck. Clouds are pinned against the Cascades and wrung out like sponges. In some of these storms, or weather events, you could be near a river and hear it and a few steps later you would hear the downpour louder than that. And you would sense that neither of them would quiet down soon enough.

Martin Egland was a hard-luck excavation contractor in the Sultan area, however, today he was over near Cathcart with his equipment when the weather converged. He really did not want to load up the gear on his trailer in this kind of weather and the November dark, when the afternoons surrender to Daylight Savings Time. He was starting to drive home in his truck, when he realized things were already happening along the shores of the rivers and he could see some lines of traffic and some emergency vehicles. He decided to go back and get on his backhoe and use some back roads to get closer to these places in the dark and see if he could provide any help. He could use an extra truck payment or two since things had turned so slow since September.

The sedimentary deposits all up and down the system were on the move. What a person usually sees when they hike these areas are the peaks of last year's movements but within a normal range. So they will more or less follow the existing curves of the river.

There is another kind of deposit that comes from an amount of material that exceeds all the normal ranges, and pretty much ignores the existing curves. These runs want to go as straight as possible and have some pretty surprising results. Over in Sequim, WA, a railroad bridge had stood for a hundred years over the bottom of the Dungeness, which has every reason to rush straight as it first leaves the foothills. It has a mere 28-hour travel-life from snowpack to ocean. And yet in a recent winter, some 5 miles from the foothills, half-way out on its delta to the ocean, a drift of water and muck and trees built up momentum during a storm. A straight run developed just upstream from the railroad bridge which had allowed for 20 feet of height over the river bed and the straight run crashed a set of pilings with trees, mud and rock, not to mention the 'spirit' of such a mudflow, water. In fiscal year 2015, it would take just over a million dollars to repair.

There are no 'tracking' devices for such incidents that would tell the locals when and where they are happening. Sometimes you just have to get out and listen and remember what your river sounded like previously and use your judgement. The worst case of all would be when you knew the mood of the river sounded *enraged.* In those cases, you'd better be moving to safety.

Martin needed money. 'The problem with being low on money is that you're low on money,' he would tell people who thought they had the ideal suggestion for him to pursue, but for which he lacked any resources or capital. He had goodwill about being out in such a storm with extra lighting and emergency flashers going; he was willing to do his part to help out neighbors. But he really wanted to land a piece of work and get reimbursed for it. To make hay while the sun shines, or move piles while the rain pours, either way.

The Snoqualmie has more meandering features than the Skykomish. The Sky already has the straighter lines which are the warning lines for the experienced.

Not that Martin knew anything about that. What he knew was that law enforcement were pressed at one curve where a slurry had rammed into the bank and attacked the road in what the local Seahawk fans would describe as 'contact outside the field of play.'

On this curve, instead of taking away the road in one of those gaping holes big enough for a truck to fall into, the slurry had piled up on top of the existing. Not that it mattered, but that's how that underlying pile came into existence, too. It was too dark to notice, of course, that the shape of pile had swollen to match the existing mound into which the road's curve had been built. The waters then formed a bit of a whirlpool on one side, but after 'finding out' how much material had deposited on this curve, and not being able to move it again, the river was turning away from the whirlpool, and moving on.

"You're at your own risk here," explained an officer from Snohomish County to Martin, "Watch your footing, I mean. Who knows what its like below you? I'm working on getting a light bank, but I might have a few flare parachutes on their way first. Thanks for your help!"

"Reminds me of trees down on the highways as a kid. My dad jumped out one night and had a tree rolled out of the way before I could even wake up from the chain saw noise!"

The base turned out to be stable enough. Martin edged away at the piled-on deposit, a scoop at a time going to the downstream bank he had approached on. Fortunately this time, there was not a guard rail to avoid, as the shape of the road's curve was land-ward.

In a half hour, one lane was open and the officers patrolled single-lane traffic for a while. It was now about 11:00 PM. The officers said there were other reports of overruns by slurries and debris, but no county roads were affected. Martin would have to find a private road that needed help. He started back to his pickup and trailer.

In the low lights of his tractor and of the oncoming cars, he started to get a sense of what these slurry flows were doing. And he knew of one community where people had built really low. 'They'll be screwed if they don't have flood insurance!' He continued that direction.

As he moved closer to that community, he could tell the bridges were still intact, but there were only odds and ends to push around, and some limbs. Then he noticed a lane piled with debris. There were 5 mailboxes at the beginning of the lane, and the cluster of receptacles had stayed intact. He started moving enough debris to give them the access they would need.

On his third scoop, there was something in the mix that was way too big to be one of the pushed over groups of alders, and way too smooth. It was too short and stout to be a tree. He rubbed off some of the silt and decided to get some water. No one was around as it was about midnight in conditions you really didn't want to be out in if you could help it. He sloshed the water on it and realized it was a fairly new and preserved wood carving, from a cedar about two foot thick, but he did not yet know the identity of the object. He decided to move as carefully as possible as it did not seem to be an amateur project.

He cleaned off everything above the piece and then he decided to try another lift from below, but with his forks. The bottom of his bucket had slide-in slots for forks for a quick alternative for moving palletized material. He cleaned all this out and inserted the forks and approached. He now realized it was very irregular because several feet to his right, something moved in the

13

mud at the same time that he lifted his end. He washed off more of his end and realized the shape was the rump of an animal of some sort, and its tail, and fairly large sized. He swung lighting over to the other end and shoveled some more. He never expected to bother with any handwork on a night light this, but here he was out in the muck, hoping now that there was money in it.

He now changed his description from irregular to delicate as he realized the remote movement were antlers. In fact, they seemed to be *actual* antlers and too big to be a large deer. It was a fairly new, professionally-carved elk.

He put a scoop back on top of it to cover it and drove away. He needed to think up a plan about this. There might be some money in it.

~ ~ ~

Michael Ostrand had memorized 19th century British geologist Lyell's PRINCIPLES OF GEOLOGY as a senior in high school. Not that he had trouble getting interested in girls and had to "bury" himself. But he then became the kind of thing the universities wish to scout for professor material—the student with the early start. So he was now professor of general theory of geology.

He had settled into some field work where Cascadia was his "lab." He'd sample cores from undergrad crews that monitored the slight movements of the Juan de Fuca or Cascadia plates of earth and study that important question: what might they do next?

He had a comfortable life. Two children with Elana Morton, his cave-woman, and a hobby ranch in the Snohomish watershed. 3 days a week on campus. Interesting young students and pretty girls. Frequent travel and conferences circulating among other geologists, most of whom were on Lyell's mission unaware.

In other areas of life, the department colleagues were only 'liberated from Moses,' Lyell would say, in a hodge-podge of ways. Many had normal families and some even attended main-denomination churches which didn't mention Genesis 1-11 if they could help it. 'It's like talking about Caspar the friendly ghost!' one of the pastors said, and had special committees policing the conversations of parishioners for anything they might say against homosexuality. You would be asked to leave the group because everyone knew they were being treated as badly as those African slaves in their 16" x 42" spaces on 18th century slave ships. Not very much else mattered morally at these churches besides fairness for that group.

Michael was in his 16th year in the geology department at the U. He basically couldn't be bothered with very much else. He had now spent 20 years "underground" mentally and it showed socially.

It was difficult to gain social accolades in geology which other disciplines enjoyed. On one hand, plate tectonics was a recently established science and he had to be content with going down in history as a pioneer among his peers. On the other hand, the big prize was an understanding of where the next Big One would hit. Making public statements about this on behalf of the U was a bit humiliating because middle school kids could basically announce the same thing and the point would be made. It would be big, and we don't know where. Then there was the additional problem of what could be done in a half second. The use of the results of studies were behind the scenes. Information would be passed on to building engineers and that was about it. Then it would be years before there was a reality test. Only a few would pay as much attention to such announcements as they would to a breakthrough on throat cancer. There was very little that could be done about the Big One.

All this had a way of reducing Michael's own appetite for life to merely rarified discoveries about tectonic plates and how they moved a mere inch per year. Research funding often came from oil companies which he didn't really relish cultivating. It was a shame to find such a small world in the geologic mantle, but there it was. Small. It was a big day when a quarter inch movement was detected in tertiary stone through the latest in acoustical metric equipment. It was a shame that it was so diminished because there were others who were finding that geo-history was part of something enormously engrossing.

So it was that Michael was now hardly interested in his children, had little appreciation of what might happen to his idyllic little farm on the Snohomish River, or what might be the motivations of hard-times working neighbors around him.

He was a child of a child of the 60s and would now rather have spent his time on flashier science like global cooling. Except that that was now global warming. Except that that was now climate change. Yes, he could be out making declarations about climate justice.

Michael and Elana never married because they couldn't figure out why that mattered. For the same reason, they never could figure out what the big deal was about the same-sex marriage 'victory.' Elana had wanted two children and had them. She wasn't even sure about that sometimes.

The geologists weren't a real warm group individually or together. Not even when the subject was 3000-degree Centigrade magma. There was an orthodoxy about what they could publish and how it would sound. You were damned if you differed. Michael sometimes wished he could get away with the nonsense the climate scientists did. But it would never happen.

Tonight, however, all of that mattered very little as the superlatives had been brought out in descriptions of this November storm. The Sno was to break records. Last week's large snowfall would all wash down, too.

There were traffic back ups out at Michael's exit. His home was not an hour from campus tonight. He began to wonder if he'd be able to make it home. He was still sitting near Woodinville and he wasn't sure if his exit off of 522 was open. It had the feel of being closed.

Law enforcement was screening people because, much to the delight of local hoteliers, they were explaining how much closure there was, and that a hotel was the best option. The option for those who waited too long would be a night in a public school gym. The other option this evening was to wait for an hourly update to come through.

After Daylight Saving's starts, the northwest moves quickly into winter with its 5 PM sunsets. Seattlites become half-Alaskan and just dive in to the dark-damp-cold. Some say this explains such strange traditions as using Tartar Sauce on french fries.

Elana called about the traffic.

"I don't know yet," answered Michael. "I don't like to call until I know something for sure... Well, make them hot chocolate and build the fire. The house is way up from that waterline. It's fine. It's the old barn I'd be concerned about... He's what? Tell him to knock if off. Tell him to go down and look at the barn for me but stay safe--where you can see him. It'll let off some pressure of his curiosity."

He really didn't like managing kids, least of all by phone. He hung up before she was done.

~ ~ ~

Everyone in the medical picture was a bit puzzled about Darcy Ostrand-Morton. She had this sensation of her extremities heating up and she had irregular blood oxygen saturation. It was a perplexing combination in that one was the reverse of the octogenarian female's sensation of cold extremities, while the other was often treated in the elderly. Darcy was resilient about doctors who could not get it solved, but most of all she wished her dad cared more. She didn't really need it solved, she just wished it mattered to him.

"Thanks for the drive today, mom," she thanked Elana. The drives. Elana didn't know what else to do. They were out one day a few months earlier and Darcy couldn't take any more heat. She'd been wading in the Sno, but they had to run errands, and her face sunk. They got in the car, and her mom went a little ways and then stopped.

"Hey, open the window behind me and lay on the back seat and put your feet out. That way they'll be up, too, like Dr. Silvers was saying."

Darcy loved it. She would start doing that everywhere they went.

16

They would pick up one of her friends and the friend would put Darcy's head up on her legs and giggle. There were faces painted on the bottom of her feet now, and she had worked out conversations between these feet-puppets about being soul-mates or about the one not having a soul and the angry response by the other about such an accusation.

"Any time I can," responded Elana, "But I don't know what it'll be like for a week now with this flooding and all these closures."

~ ~ ~

At 1:30am, Elana ripped off her blankets and yelled "No!...No!" It was that moment before being awake when the intensity of her voice was getting ahead of things. She threw on her robe, and grabbed a flashlight, looking out the first window she could open. It was angry and noisy and raining hard. But that wasn't the direction to look. She went out to the deck and felt the rain invade her slippers as she looked down the driveway. It seemed normal, she couldn't be sure.

'It was a nightmare' she told herself. 'Or was it? Ohh,' she groaned, 'And what can I do about it?'

The vivid dream had it that the driveway had been chewed away, and since it dropped down 20 feet as it neared the river, that meant they were on an island, until something temporary was fixed, and that meant some weeks without trips for Darcy and a whole barrage of inconvenience. She was flooded with troubles and upset that Michael was gone and she could not get an official report from him about the lane.

She couldn't sleep and was tired of hearing the rain.

They were children of hippies, devotees of the earth, and through Michael's position at the U, they had money. Michael was hardly there as a parent, however. It was all Elana. It was Elana who knew the parameters of the river if it acted up. Sometimes she simply couldn't figure out how Michael was such an expert, yet seemed to have no grasp of what the river might do. She was not aware that that is what 'specialist' might some day mean. She sometimes had brutal questions for him which he never answered. She remembered how evasive he was when he mentioned being consulted by a NOVA writer about north America's surface being 'built.' He had the uniformitarian view that was simply that each layer was once the surface. This was entirely predictable, all the way down.

"So does it grow like an onion—thickening layer by layer?" asked Elana.

"Well, no, of course not. It's not a plant."

"So how does soil grow?"

"Organic material accumulates on top in entirely predictable succession."

"Entirely predictable? Didn't you see what they were talking about down at the Grand Canyon on that trip?"

"Oh, that's all amateur material for the masses."

"No it's not; that's the official word on how that place emerged. Those were national park murals and dioramas, and there was a huge area where 275 million years was missing in the layering. And then there was all that foreign sediment..."

"*Non-conforming,*" he corrected clerically.

"What?"

"The sediment was non-conforming."

"But how can that be? You just said it was uninterrupted accumulation. Anyway, remember when *we* were non-conforming? What's the matter with that?"

"I did, but they are not worth chasing down. You have to stick with the logical progression or you're wasting time or oil company money or government funding. We were *socially* non-conforming. Not about this kind of thing. This is set in, well, stone."

"But I've also listened to all those experts tell us that the glaciers are receding. But we visited Taku Glacier Lodge. And guess when Hole-in-The-Wall grew? During the middle of the 20th century! So I asked one of the 'experts' at the U what that means, and he said Taku was 'insensitive' to warming! I mean, with 'science' like that, it is no wonder Obama went up there and made his fool remarks."

"What is that about?"

"He knew Muir said that Glacier Bay was ice-free as far back as 1900 and yet Obama was concerned that global warming was due to 20th century industry—when Taku grew Hole-in-the-Wall, which is larger than some of those glaciers which have disappeared, even though it is only a finger of Taku. I think I'm going to be 'insensitive' about some of this stuff. Anyway, what happened to Bretz, then? Why did geologists put away his work on the Lake Missoula deluge for a decade?"

"Another word for it is *anomaly,* but look, the NOVA program has a script, and they want an efficient way to express what happened. You can't waste your time on rabbit trails and you can't waste a producer's budget on exceptions."

In spite of these professional explanations, Elana was becoming more and more suspicious. She didn't even watch the NOVA special even though Michael would be listed in the credits. It was way too much logical theory for her and life was not logical. There were all kinds of exceptions to accept and master and the emotions that came along with them. She was actually not sure Michael felt very much of anything these days. Was his science the next

18

one to turn 'insensitive' in to a positive trait?

For his part, Michael was seriously wondering what women were for. If he was working by himself in his core sample room and had a thought come to him, did his woman-partner know?

~ ~ ~

Michael stayed around his hotel as long as they allowed, but there still was no bulletin on the WA DOT site about the rest of 522. He thought about the straight view of the Cascades at the property when he first saw it 12 years ago, but he had no idea now how those same site-lines were paths of destruction. In those same channels, a mud slurry could pick up quite a bit of force and seriously alter a property description. Michael's mind was underground, professionally. He actually didn't "concern" himself with what was seen out on the surface; he was much more involved in what could be conceptualized about the layers of materials below, analyzed in core samples from exotic spots.

It was 4 PM by the time his area of river bottom developments was open to the public again. That was also all the sooner he had called Elana. Will had had nothing to report about the barn, or it was too dark to tell. When Michael turned into their lane, something else was wrong.

At first he saw Will, and by coincidence Will had not gone down this far and noticed what was wrong either. They found out at the same time.

"Get in" Michael called. "Let's go downstream and check."

Michael had driven in as usual from upstream, but he could tell there had been some pounding and sloshing at the foot of his drive by a restless river. It just never occurred to him that an expensive cedar carved elk could have been shoplifted on its angry way.

"I can't believe it." He really couldn't and he didn't ask how Will's night was or Darcy or their mother. He just drove slowly and looked for clues in the late, shadowy light.

"I didn't even look this way" Will offered, as though dad might be angry for not checking.

Michael was silent. His mathematical mind had remembered to press the trip miles button back at the driveway. They were about a mile away and he only had a few "suspects"--piles of debris or new piles of gravel that could be interrogated. He got out and stopped to look over one knot of trees and clay and some trash about 30 yards away. "It's going to be like the game of hidden pictures, Will. How are we going to do this? There's so many shapes there that could be the one."

~ ~ ~

Amanda Reese had taken her bike to work lately because the morning after the Snohomish storm started she and her 4 neighbors found their river acreage lane partially-blocked and no taxis available, and rumors of blockages all over. But the store was open. She needed the money and so she biked in and covered other people's shifts.

On that first morning she saw some tractor tracks but she didn't think about it. But it was the following morning that she noticed even more tracks and that the lane was call clear. She recalled something unusual her mother had said.

"I was up in the night to make a stop and I saw some flickering lights down there, at the road. I could see a bright yellow sign. There's no bright yellow signs down there, are there?"

"Well, it must have been an emergency crew."

Amanda went down the lane to look around and returned satisfied that an emergency crew had come and opened their lane.

"What time was it?" she said returning into the kitchen.

"Midnight. It's always midnight for me when I make my trip."

"I suppose they work whenever or wherever the river has died down. Anyway, it was our turn to get some clean up, I guess, and it's done. So now...if I can just find out if our road is open or find out about driving around on that one they paved last year..."

~ ~ ~

Martin worked eBay and Craigslist for the Bay area and then the Reno—Tahoe area. He set up an enticing entry:

FOR SALE BY OWNER
LANDSCAPE décor

CEDAR ELK
REAL ANTLERS
HAND-CARVED, NOT CHAIN-SAW ART
TWO-TONED PRESERVED DISTRESSED CEDAR
LIFE-SIZE
SHIPPING INCLUDED (BUT NOT OFF-LOADING)
UNIT IS IN HARNESS READY FOR OFF-LOADING
FOOTING NEEDS RECONSTRUCTION
$15,000 OR OFFER

"Bank." He consoled himself. "There's got to be that much there." He had checked with a lumber store for the term 'distressed' and believed he was on the right track.

~ ~ ~

Martin had Jeff set up a phone number in northern California. The calls forwarded through from his online ad directed to the general Bay area. "I'm calling about the carved cedar elk."

"Yes," answered Martin only a few hours later. He'd made a note of the area codes and it was Marin County. "Would you like to see it? It's in the vehicle and I can probably reach you in a couple hours."

"Yes, let's have a look. Sounds fantastic. I've got a redwood grotto, you see. The theme is the force of nature, so, yeah, an alpha-male elk would fit right in. Even better if it had a broken-off antler—the struggle to dominate, you know."

"Perfect" said Martin, in the most two-faced declaration he'd ever uttered in his life.

~ ~ ~

"Jeff? Where are you?" Jeff was comfortably settling into some serious kissing with his girlfriend at an exit north of Sacramento where there appeared to be decent turn off to the Bay Area. They were waiting for the first call from Martin.

"Well, I was looking at I-5 here down near Sacramento and trying to find the optimum place to cut over either way, so I'm just here on I-5."

"OK, OK, so we're going to Marin County north of Golden Gate. So let's see, I've got to call him back with an exit to call back to you. He's got a landscaper working on a grotto or something, and he's sending him over to see the merchandise. I don't think you can transfer there, but he'll know the next step if they go ahead. Meanwhile, I'll get another client lined up, in case."

"This is fun. Is this a new line you're pursuing? It's a nice break from all the other torture you put me through, ha, ha. And Stacey's having fun, too."

"It's...just a spare opportunity that came up at just the right time, alright?" Something sounded tense to Jeff.

"Hey, boss. I didn't mean anything."

"I know, I know."

"What's going on? You don't sound like yourself."

"Well, that's something that's off limits, OK? You just let me decide what 'myself' is."

"Yeah, yeah. I'll get off and let you find the interchange. Bye." Jeff hung up.

"What? What's the matter?" asked Stacey, trying to get close again.

21

"He doesn't sound good... Anyway, he'll be calling back in a minute with the exact interchange where we meet a client, a landscaper."

"I like to snuggle" breathed Stacey into Jeff's ear.

"I can tell."

"I mean, I'd rather cuddle, especially when you're out working, too. It's so yum."

Jeff couldn't put all that together, except that he never bought into the genders being identical, but then his phone rang. "That was quick." He tapped. "Hello?"

"OK, so he says take the 505 down to the 80 and go to the Bay Area to the Cordelia exit, which is also where 680 will start. There's an Azteca Restaurant there, and his guy is in Marinwood. And he says call when you get to the 80. It's real simple. Call when you get to the 80 and you'll be at the Cordelia exit at the same time."

"Got it. Stacey's already put it into her phone and map, so we're on our way."

They pulled into the 505 stream.

"I'm just saying remember that when you're older" added Stacey. "You know--" she looked over to see if he was looking her in the eye-- "When we have kids. I mean, you've at least thought about it, haven't you? About kids? I'm just saying I want to snuggle. It's like your charger."

Jeff had that look in his eye like he was not thinking about having kids. The look rehearsed past troubles with parents, but he was getting even with those parents...by being harsh on kids who had not even been born yet.

"Charger?"

"That box, in your garage... The 'Tickle..."

"Oh, *trickle* charger. The slow overnight battery charger."

"Yeah, I mean, I just want to trickle-charge by snuggling with you. I know men and women are wired different. Ha, ha. *Wiring!* See! I just need a trickle-charge. I don't need what you need the same way. I'll need my trickle charges, and if I don't get them, I won't want to give you yours."

"That's honest. And clear. Let's keep it that way."

Stacey smiled. And thought she'd said about all he could take about that topic for one day. He'd say something like 'please stop talking.'

"Please stop talking."

So Stacey was now bummed but enjoyed the total change in scenery that kept coming toward her, mile after mile. "It's 70 degrees out here!" she exclaimed. But inside she was debating whether she wanted a boyfriend or a husband.

~ ~ ~

22

The drive took them down the Sacramento River and they could see the Bay Area taking shape. At the Azteca meeting spot, the landscaper was on the phone several minutes hopping up into the van to check it out. It was a go. Jeff made sure of payment before moving on, talking to Martin again.

The next drive rose into the hills north of the bay where they ducked as windmills swung overhead. They wound up in a spread with Pacific and Bay views where Jeff couldn't even imagine the market value. He was glad he was arriving in a new-looking vehicle instead of his trickle-mobile.

The creature was carefully extracted and laid down by the front-end loader of the landscaper's crew.

"Now this is really a find. It's really worth shuffling a few things around here. Alright, what we're going to do is try the color in our sunset. That hint of maroon. Wow. I've got to see that in actual sunlight, in conditions here, so yeah, let's get over there. I've never bagged an elk before!" He pointed the trac driver to a horizon line. "I'd like them to see it when they drive home."

The next stretch of work went on for a couple hours. Jeff was explaining certain features. The question came up as to how such a thing was found. He didn't know, he said, it was something his boss acquired and he knew very little. "They weren't interested with the broken footing to deal with. They gave it to him simply for retrieving it." The landscaper had traveled too far into the aesthetics of using the piece to be truly concerned. Neither of them thought like a detective.

In the next moment, Jeff shuddered because he had never really asked Martin how he got the rights to the carving. He was about 10 years younger than Martin and just assumed that it was as he just told the customer. A spike of doubt came over him and he was not a professional at hiding emotion from a customer. There now was a piece missing. He quickly looked into the van, partly to see if it was loose in there, and partly to hide his face from the buyer in case it had turned extremely white. A right antler tip was broken off fresh and missing. The third. It was not in the truck.

The landscape crew didn't think about the significance of this, but for Jeff it was a bother. He was plagued by whether a piece of evidence like that was going to matter to Martin. He didn't know. He didn't know when it happened. He was worried about how he would tell Martin.

"Well, thanks again."

Jeff pushed out a smile and dropped the freight door on the van. He had just assumed the entire time that Stacey was milling around the estate or sitting in the truck on her phone or something. He wasn't going to tell her. He didn't know what he was going to do about it. He was distracted with calculating what would happen if he didn't say anything. To Martin. But that was eclipsed by yet another problem.

She was nowhere to be found.

Jeff and the crew called around the hilly grounds. She was not there.

After 10 minutes, Jeff didn't believe this was happening and dove into the calls he now needed to make to Martin, to figure out what next. Actually, for Jeff, it was perfect. Now he didn't need to mention the missing antler piece. Who would be concerned about an antler piece like that when a young woman, 20s, blond, was missing?

Martin sounded like he was helping Jeff out about Stacey, but secretly he thought this was "perfect." So his two-faced declaration earlier was now not enough. Nothing would be a bigger distraction from the stolen elk than Stacey's disappearance. Who would be concerned about where this carved elk came from when a young woman was missing?

"So what are you going to do, Jeff? I need that van turned in and I've got work for you here. I could find someone else, but I'd rather not. You can file a report, but they won't do anything for days. I've got the money for your tickets... Call her and tell her to get to Oakland International... I don't know... I don't know her that well."

"She hasn't answered for over an hour."

2

CONVERSATIONS

"Why *do* you have a background in geology?" Michael asked Cam Berra. Sargeant Berra was a field detective for the Snohomish County Sherriff. It was his CO's opinion that this hunt for the carved elk would be just right for him to take up. His office window looked out on the Snohomish floodplain and up to the Cascades.

"I started out looking into catastrophes."

"Katrina?"

"No, larger. Global, geologic."

"What are you talking about?"

"Massive flooding in accounts from most cultures. Hundreds of them. Not hundreds of floods, but hundreds of accounts with similar features. What you might call 'unnecessarily' similar details. Sometimes you can't tell if they mean the creation of the world or not. But I didn't dwell on that, I tried, anyway, to stick to the mechanics, the hydrology, the physics.

"I questioned the whole concept of 'nonconforming' geology. When I realized that there are patterns in the sand where a river runs into the sea, and that you can find the same patterns in the Palouse, seen from space, I tried to study how the same soil movements could happen. Pretty soon I noticed 'Grand Canyons' out where there is plenty of sand and the tide can come over all of it twice a day."

"But now you're in this—investigations, detective work, forensics."

"I was at the U and they weren't real interested in where I was going. They said there was no career in it. There were some rumors about what happened to Bretz, and when I met my wife, I didn't want to have to fight uphill and 'undo' the UW geology department, so I picked out something that to me was similar, and paid me enough, but you might be surprised why I thought it was similar. It was still physics but on a smaller scale."

"What would surprise me?"

"It's a conversation between a literature scholar at Oxford and a uniformitarian."

Michael stiffened as though he had just heard a banned expression or at least a very rare one. "What are you talking about?"

"It was Lewis—the same gentleman who wrote the SPACE TRILOGY and who married an American Communist gal who got cancer right away so they only had a couple years together. Her son helped orchestrate that top-quality production of NARNIA back in 2006, which was some of the children's material Lewis wrote...

"Anyway he had this conversation which he wrote up as an essay called 'Religion and Science.' The scientist told him why all miracles were a worthless trail to pursue, a thing of a distant past's world of fantasy. Lewis told him a story about coins that a person keeps accumulating in the office drawer. It goes something like this:

"So, for whatever reason, let's say every day you are putting one nickel in your top drawer, day after day. It's entirely predictable. You can extrapolate out that 10 days from now there will be 10 more coins there. That projecting-out, said Lewis, was how the 19th and 20th century uniformitarian viewed Nature. The scientists are like mathematicians, calculating out as far as needed to tell us what Nature will or won't do. Unless something were to interrupt it. *Provided that nothing happens* was the exact expression he used."

"So what?" remarked Michael.

"Right. He went on to explain that if 5 were missing one day, or 8 dimes were added, or the whole desk were gone one day, then you'd have an *un-natural* event. Those scientists would be in a tizzy, because nothing ever happens in their view, except the collecting of dust—and coins. "Un-natural" would mean super-natural or miracle. Most important: it would not be in the mathematicians' realm. Lewis said the scientist who is busy at his work observing Nature can only tell us how many coins there will be on day x, or y. But if you want to explain an unnatural event, you wouldn't ask *him.* You'd find a psychologist or a detective or maybe a psychic. That's when I realized—I was a *detective*, but I was doing geology. I wanted to do it but keep an eye out for unexpected forces."

"I see. You mean he said that scientists were stuck in a limited set of explanations?"'

"Kind of. They only had a few kinds of answers and they had all got together and ruled out several other things. I couldn't accept that; I couldn't accept that looking at the things I saw in the Cascades or in the eastern

Washington scablands, etc. Or the landscape and artefacts at Naszca. I couldn't rule things out the way they did.

"Actually, at that point I became a *psychologist* because the question of why they would do that was now more vital than the next geologic 'find.' Or you might say I was now a detective in the thought-world of people who were said to be telling us the truth about the geologic story."

"Then I found out about Bretz and how they—geologists!--ruled out a whole decade of his work. I found out the Jenkins collection about Naszca was top secret and extremely complicated to access. I found out almost nothing sensible is out there in the literature about the thousands of standing dead mammoths in the north, or that these 'scientists' won't answer any questions Graham Hancock puts up. You probably thought I was just based on Genesis alone, but actually..."

None of which Michael wanted to hear about. "So what are you going to do for me?"

"Well, nothing. Nothing *active*." Cam knew how badly that sounded and that Michael had probably heard quite enough for one session. For one thing, Michael's ears had turned red and his eyes were darting all over. "We're in the process-of-elimination phase."

"What does that mean?"

"There are miles of runs of slurry now that were never there before in the Sno. We don't even have aerial photographs yet. We don't know what the main impacts of this storm were compared to the existing plain. We can't just go poking around through the piles, even with the logical limitation of the most immediate beds downstream from you. Wood has a funny way of moving, and this was dry cedar. There are also the logarithms about the relocation of objects relative to the amount of force that strikes them in fluid dynamics. We don't have that measured yet, really. It has its antlers and is likely to hang up in a tree on a crest of a swell rather than get buried. It's far less predictable than sediment. Some of these piles aren't even safe yet anyway. They settle, collapse, sink into logpiles.

"What we have to do is wait for people to get out and about and call in about the unusual things they find. It goes on for weeks, and people find these things and say 'Bet the flood put that car there' or 'there's Melanie's clawfoot tub over there!'

"I remember one of my first drives through the area. I had been through the Toutle area after Mount St. Helens and you could see all the Corps work moving the sediment and ash around with bellyscrapers. But when I drove through here, I had to keep reminding myself that there was no Corps work going on. These were just rock-flows or slurries and at various logjams or rockpiles, there might be a sudden breach and pow! You'd have another mini-flood inside the main flooding and it would barge right into anything in its way.

"What I mean is we have to kind of let go, but also think outside the box. 'Let go' means we can't start prodding around the nearest piles downstream. 'Outside the box' means, like Lewis, that it's not just a matter of knowing floods. You have to know people, too. What's the thing law enforcement dreads most when there a disaster like this?"

"Are you talking about looting?"

"Kind of. But what would you call it when someone takes advantage of just one item like this, and otherwise everyone is civil and honest? You see, it's more insidious than looting because it is more unthinkable. Looting is class war, and it wasn't the rich classes that caused the damage. That's where the detective part comes in. So you should let us do our work and let time take its course."

"OK..." Michael got up to leave. He was mad. He was not just mad about having Cam assigned to this question but about people who looted. He hated people mostly, and this kind of thief a lot. "Do you do *any* geology anymore?"

"I do."

"Oh, yeah? Like what?"

"I do presentations on CTP. Catastrophic plate tectonics. The first paper about it was in 1986. I'm working on an animation with a woman who has a background in it—in animation--from her time in LA but now she's a graphics designer up here in Everett."

"About the Cascades?"

"The animation? No, no. It's global. But I've been to Mount St. Helens area several times to work on the model. So Cascadia is involved."

"How do you mean? St. Helens is an anomaly."

"I mean there's data from Monterey Canyon. Monument Valley. The Beijing Anomaly. The Nordic Deluge legend. The Centralia theory."

Michael was stumped enough to find himself out in a little county sheriff deputy's office being told to sit back about the carving, but now he was flummoxed to have been handed a list by this part-time geologist that he really didn't ever talk about, under a heading he never used, and about which he had almost nothing to say. Yet back at his office, he had an original copy of Lyell's PRINCIPLES which he'd brought back from Siccar Point, Scotland, himself and, for all practical purposes, had memorized. Finally, he made an overture.

"Well, when is the next time you'll be showing this—*animation*?" he asked with definite condescension accenting the word 'animation.'

There was good reason for this, but Michael misunderstood one important angle. Animations and simulations of climate change abounded but were so erroneous as to be little boys crying wolf. Or they ended up with so little change that it was an embarrassment. But they all had one thing in common: they were about the *future*. Cam was re-enacting something from the *past*. All that could happen as research continued was that it would get closer and closer to reality.

"Shara has access to a studio downtown Seattle by KOMO and about once a month she'll go down, rent some time and have me stop by at the end of her hours there to see what she's got. It's a private-funded project. But--sorry--to answer you more clearly, there is a presentation in 2 weeks. I'd love to have you come, get your impressions, questions. Or I could make you a copy of it as is."

Michael left the office, but he wasn't completely persuaded to leave the investigation alone. He thought he'd get his son involved in some tracking and mapping practice. But first he went back to the sheriff.

"Do you have a minute?"

"Indeed. Come, have a seat."

"That detective—Berra?"

"Top notch."

"Really? The guy is a freakin' fundamentalist who thinks there is a young earth and a massive worldwide flood actually took place. You know those plastic bath tub toys of Noah's Ark and all that drivel? All based on a book that thinks the stars are, what, a mile up? That's what he's about. He got kicked out of geology, you know."

"He's been on board 8 years now and he's a sharp as Foyle."

"Foyle?"

"FOYLE'S WAR? You've never heard of the British detective series who always has those triple cases to detangle?"

"So he does alright, you're saying?"

"Top notch."

"Well, don't be surprised when I walk in with some information that my own guy has found."

"Your son?"

"Private agency. I don't mean a detective. I just mean an excavator. Or both."

The sheriff gasped. "If I thought that was needed, I'd have let you know. It's best if you lay low and let the things that matter show up on their own in these things. That's why we didn't assign anyone the first week. People get careless and talk. There's probably drugs involved. It's probably a druggie who wanted to make some quick money. But we don't even know if *someone* is involved yet. If you go out there with an excavator, besides the risk of a debris-pile collapse—you know, Oso was a collapse that just needed water to happen—there's the risk of some criminal knowing how to cover up what he's done. We have procedures and you need to let them do their work.

I really wish you wouldn't. It raises a profile and if there is someone involved out there, he'll start doing artificial things—overkill, coverups, etc. Just let it go and the right details will bubble up to the surface at the right time. And, anyway, now we know this is partly a *geological* mystery.

"You see, Cam's an unusual combination of skill sets and he'll be very valuable right now. He checked into a lot of things up at Oso. The speed and distance- measurements and so on because it was really saturated. How else would a person get to see a 6- to 800 foot mound of sedimentary go into action?"

"I'll think about it. What's his interest in *that*?"

"Oh... It doesn't sound like you've talked. He might solve something about Oso, but I suppose the greatest mystery, in his book, is the Yellow Band."

"The what?"

"Near the top of Everest. The huge layer of rapid deposit sediment near the top. Here..." He clicked around on his keyboard. "Like the Australian geologist asks, 'How do you get several hundred feet of rapid deposit sediment from across the continent up that high?" He showed Michael an image.

"Why rapid?"

"Hydrology. Fluid dynamics. If you move it slow, it looks one way. If you move it fast, it looks another. If you move it across a continent quickly, it looks one way. I don't think there's a way to move it that far slowly. It has to move quick, because you're fighting gravity. This is what they are saying about Pluto, you know. It may be why they are saying it is 'not a planet'—it's too *young*. Exactly what we deal with in forensics. Accident scenes. If you moved that hillside in Oso.."

"OK, OK." Michael was irritated. Here was a county sheriff presiding over thousands of Boeing engineers and he was another lunatic who didn't know about millions of years, or didn't seem to! He closed it out. "Have a good day."

"Can I ask you one other thing?" the sheriff closed.

"Go ahead."

"In your own words, what makes you so energized to find this? Is it the amount of money you have in it?" The sheriff needed to know his real drive and motivation.

"Look, I just don't think it could have gone that far. If nothing has broken off, and it's still in one piece, then I want to get to it and get it cleaned up as soon as I can."

The sheriff shrugged. "Fair enough. Have a good day."

3

ANIMATIONS

After a few weeks, when the storm and the loss of the carving were a bit in the past, Michael arrived home from the U one afternoon to find Elana driving out of the lane with Darcy's bare feet hanging out the window behind her.

"What are you off to? Do you want me to take her now, and you can stay home?"

Elana backed up quickly and got out. She got out of the car and went inside without a word. Darcy was crying. Michael parked his car and got in.

"Is there anything you need, Darc?"

"Just go. Get Tamara first. Wait, mom said she had to get to Walgreen's. You better check."

Michael was on the outside when it came to helping Darcy. He really didn't know what was going on.

"No, there's nothing" answered Elana. "I have to talk to some people. I have to go talk to a pharmacist, I think. Just go enjoy some time out with her." She went to the pantry and poured a glass of wine.

Michael took her along the river. He was amazed at the long runs of gravel bars.

"Just keep moving for a while, dad. When you slow down, there's warm air from the car, and I can feel it."

"I'm looking at the gravel bars and sand piles because the carving could be out there anywhere."

"There's piles and piles, dad. I don't see how you'll ever find it."

"I'm going to start at the house and work downstream. I think a quick look through the trees will eliminate whether the antlers got caught in them, but if they broke off, then its a total loss, damn it."

"Dad...why do you care so much about it?"

31

"It cost a lot. And then there is the artist's beliefs. You know, when a music band wants to do another version of some musician's song, they have to get his permission. Because there is sort of spirit to it. Well, in the carver's beliefs, it's more than that. He says the elk—or actually the cedar tree--is an ancestor and so losing the carving is about how I'm treating his ancestor."

"Really. I don't get that. I mean I didn't know you thought that mattered. It's religious, dad. And you said you weren't. But more than that. The *river* did it. So why do we have to protect a piece of wood? What if another native's ancestor is the *river* and the river came and ruined this carving? Then whose ancestor are we supposed to respect?"

"You're very smart, Darcy." He preferred not to have his 'beliefs' examined. Or anyone's, as far as that goes. It was supposed to be 'faith' and 'faith' was not supposed to make any sense. It was all supposed to be more detached and theoretical than that. He was going to tell her she was ruining it for him. Had he really known Darcy, he would have known that though her hypoxia often affected her memory and other mental processes, she had bursts where she fought back and made extremely brilliant deductions, and he had just witnessed one superior to anything even Elana had ever heard.

"Thanks."

They were silent for a while. Darcy was doing well enough to sit up.

"I can get carsick doing this, at least I think that's what it is. But dad, I don't remember anything you did for me until we accidentally met in the driveway and my feet were out. Is that what it takes to get your attention—I have to have my feet hanging out of a car?"

Darcy cried.

Michael reached back to hold her hand, but she pulled back.

"I just want to feel good, dad."

Michael was going to react badly but he caught himself. *She's just a kid*, he reminded himself. "Darc, did you know there's a way to take a 'mint' for your tummy without actually taking a mint?"

Darcy shook her head like she was hearing something really annoying.

"Just think the most positive thing that you can, especially if it's about a person around you. Otherwise they take over and you waste all your energy on something you can't change. Find the upside. It soothes the stomach, the inside." It was uncharacteristic for Michael to venture on to such topics. But he felt outdone by what his brilliant daughter just noticed. He didn't even practice this himself, but he knew how to say it. It came off rather well.

His mind had almost no place for learning anything about parenting. Or even for any volatile geological situations near the surface of the earth. He had spent years—or was it millions of years!--deep underground, in the tertiaries, in the -zoics. It was God's grace to him that he was ever interested in Elana at all, or had children at all. It was God's grace to Darcy that he had advised about things you can't change. Completely in spite of himself. Left to himself he would stayed been deep in Lyell's earth and never come up for air.

"Yeah?"

"Yeah."

"I'll try."

~ ~ ~

"What did he say when you asked that?" inquired Cam about Michael's incredulity that first day about the elk case, when he blasted the sheriff for having put a 'fundamentalist' on the case.

"'I just don't think it could have gone that far' was what he said."

"Well, of course, that would be true if all the forces involved are settled. But we don't know that. And if there's human forces involved... But I know the carving. I've seen it several times. I remember when it was featured in SEATTLE LIVING. I like it, too. So I'm interested in seeing it brought back."

"It would be good to let him know. I don't know what it is but there's just something antagonistic there, and we need to do anything we can to get on his side."

"Next time we talk."

"And one other thing" continued the sheriff.

"What's that?"

"He hasn't heard about Ptolemy's universe. They really buried it, didn't they?"

"Oh—so you read that article?"

"The early modern uniformitarians buried what Ptolemy said about the earth being a tiny mathematical point almost lost in a huge universe. If they admitted he knew that back then, there would be less effect of scientists coming out now and 'snowing' the world with their universe that is infinitely bigger than the Bible—they think. The ancients knew back in their day."

"You've obviously done your homework!"

"Cam, you're allowed to say that about my reading about the history of science, but you better not say that about an active case!"

They laughed together.

~ ~ ~

"Single Vision Graphics—this is Shara."

"It's Cam. Hey, something interesting has happened at work."

"Shoot."

Shara had this feeling that something intriguing would break sometime from this work with Cam. She knew him from UW days, but she left

33

for graphics design work and animation. Now she was back in the northwest and married and had children but they were at the same church. Her husband was from LA but loved it up here in the Northwest. He worked in computers. She worked from the house. They had decided a while back that there had to be a parent for the kids all through their years. There wouldn't be someone *else* raising them. She was quite happy to work about half-time from the house and be there for anything their kids needed.

She was doing her best to keep up with Cam. He'd bring over diagrams he'd found or email other videos about this topic to try to put together a coherent statement about CTP and what would have happened to plates that moved vertically and rapidly during the Genesis deluge. She'd tried a number of things. One of them was a cutaway view of an apple developing in time-lapse. Then an acorn squash. Then an acorn.

"A geology professor lives out here. I mean he is at the U and been on board there several years. I must have just missed him in my foray there, but anyway, he was just recently in my office at the county because he has lost an expensive elk carving from his yard, due to the Skykomish River."

"The flood."

"Right. We kept talking and he found out I started out in geology and when we got to the end of his questions about how I'd investigate his carving, he asked me what I was doing in geology these days, if anything. I rattled off some topics and he looked kind of vacant, like I wasn't speaking in English or something."

"Cool. So I bet you want to know if I've done anything on that animation. I hope you won't laugh but I've been working on lava lamps."

"Lava lamps. OK. And what?"

"It turns out there are already temperature and volume simulations for them and I had to find out how similar these were to the granitic magma simulator. You know, that's the one that the British guy used and said if the right vertical shaft aligned, that Yosemite's domes could form in 5 hours. Been there?"

"Yosemite? No. But I know the pictures, I mean I know what you mean about the domes."

"Now, did I have that done for your last presentation? You know, it's a segment where it zooms in? It's kind of cool—pardon the pun—because it's not the easiest thing for the mind to think about how a whole sphere morphs at a time; it's better for a person—a student—to take one thing like El Torres in Patagonia or the Yellowstone Caldera and say 'watch this model of how it likely came to have the form we see today.'"

"I...don't know—I mean if you showed that to me last time. But I like your zoomed extra segments, that's awesome. Well, back to this professor, he's interested in coming to a presentation in a couple weeks. What do you

34

think? When is your next workup downtown? Or what do you think would be ready?"

"Hmmm."

"It doesn't matter. In fact, I don't want to convey any smugness or arrogance about this, I just want him to see the Genesis texts and their echoes worked out visually and see what he says. I don't really care how finished they are. Let's just render an edition and use it. It's more important to catch some kind of misconception now and fix it, because then I can say, 'The main seismologist, etc., at the U made this criticism—blah, blah, blah—and here's how we included it.' It's stronger."

"Yeah. That's good. That's *really* good. OK, so I'll go get a DVD burnt off of the file down there and a few little touches I can do this week. Maybe one more of the zoomed segments."

~ ~ ~

After the presentation of the CPT approach which Michael gave at a church, he gave Michael his own copy.

"Granted, it's under construction."

"Yeah, yeah. Hey could we talk about the elk for a bit?"

They moved to a private room.

"You're moving like a glacier on this."

"Except, in your case, it must seem to be moving like tectonic plates, right?"

"OK, OK. But show me when you're going to get something done."

"Well, I'd be wandering off the topic a bit here, but I was under the impression that you thought slow processes were good. But don't you remember what the sheriff said about a low profile about this? People start talking, and word travels fast."

"So you've got something then?"

"I can't say, but do you know why you want to 'fix' the problem—I mean in a way that has to do with Genesis?"

"Not really. It's probably just another one of your one-liners."

"There's something in us that wants to take something that is in disarray and in a mess, and we want to make it useful."

"You think there is something in Genesis about *that*?"

"Well, that's right there in the opening scene, Michael."

"The opening scene?"

"The very first scene of Genesis. As the 'curtain' rises, the earth is formless and empty. By the end of the first 'scene' of the account, it is formed and full of life, and man is there in that same image, in fact, he's told to... Michael, can I just ask: have you ever just read it for yourself on a quiet morning, no heat

35

of debate, etc.?"

"No."

"Hmm. Well, what do you think about coalification. How long is that process?"

Michael wasn't sure what he had changed gears for, but answered the question.

"Coalification? That's more or less 150 million."

"So you don't know about the 'deafening silence' after the radiohalo tests at the Price, Utah, coal mines? He put the results in SCIENCE and GEOTIMES magazines back in the 70s."

"And what?"

"A few millenia."

"*Millenia.* That's one of your Bible words. Forget it."

"I mean in the *mathematical* sense. A thousand. It only takes a few thousand years, but time is only one of the factors. There's weight, pressure, radioactivity, vegetation density. Ever heard of any massive events that would have impacted the Colorado Plateau that would have factored into that? Did you know the Toltec, in Mexico, said that it was 1720 years from creation to the deluge? They were part of the Mayans—pretty good timekeepers, you know. That's a deluge account again where a family of 8 goes through it all by making a huge vessel. They called him 'Coxcox,' but I haven't heard how that translates out..."

"There you go again about your Genesis flood bilge. You really don't know science, do you?"

"Better than Obama at Glacier Bay in the summer of 2015! Do you know he quoted Hume, thinking it supported--"

Michael cut in. "I've waited long enough. I'm getting an excavator."

Cam held his tongue. And let go of trying to change Michael.

~ ~ ~

"Is this Excel-Land Excavating? My name is Michael."

"Yes, this is Martin at Excel-land."

"Ok. You said it so fast, I thought you said 'Excellent.' Uhh, a bit unusual. You remember the storm in November, the big mudwashes that came down?"

"Yeah, sure, I helped where I could, but people still didn't pay."

"Well, I'll pay, no worry. I'm a professor in geology at the U. But it's not about new construction. Or research. Instead, it's just that I lost something in that storm."

"In the mudflow?"

"Yeah."

"So you need to me to go poking around in the piles...OK. Just a minute." Martin put down the phone and got a huge glass of water. "Just thirsty. Sorry. OK. What are we talking about? What are we looking for?"

"Well, it's a special carving you see. I knew this Skykomish man—the tribe I mean, not the town--who was quite a carver, no chain saws, just natural native methods, because the piece of wood had the spirit of an ancestor in it, so you couldn't violate it. Of course, now it's all violated anyway, so I'm not telling you how you have to search for it, I mean, assuming you have modern machinery and all that..."

"Are we talking about cedar, then?"

"Yeah, cedar. Preserved. A full-size elk. A beautiful piece. Two-tone preservation for the mantle. And then he set real antlers there. Now that's quite a mechanic, you know, when you can carve something like that, mount antlers, and it still doesn't show! Then there was the bolts for the legs from underneath; mastercraftsman. So I need you to start from our driveway and work your way downstream—wherever they'll let you."

Martin couldn't take any more. What in the world? His mind flooded with the possibility of a trap, a decoy customer set up by the police. He couldn't think. But then he set up an escape hatch. He postponed.

"OK. Let's do this... I've got a bid on resetting a one-lane bridge and I've got to get it out by 3:00 today. Let me take your number. I'm definitely at work in the type of material you're talking about here—that's why I'm resetting the bridge. And, I see that it's the family treasure, and all that. So I'll call you back when this other pot is not boiling so hard. Will that be OK?"

"Sure, sure. It's just that I don't see where the police are doing anything about it, or they've got their hands full, so I'd like to help them by 'doing some homework,' you see. I'm at..."

Martin read the phone number back and closed the call. That line about 'I don't see where the police are doing anything about it' was exquisite. He felt relief at surviving his first round in what could only be described as 'paradox management.'

~ ~ ~

After one interview with Cam, his business card was on the Ostrand kitchen table. Elana decided to call because she wanted to know more about the simulation about catastrophes.

"Cam, this is Elana Morton. I'm Michael Ostrand's partner—different name."

"Right, right. Hi. What's new?"

"Well, I'm calling about the simulation or whatever."

"It's coming along. There's a friend in animation who is working it over. You see, it is sort of like those 3D animations of a V8 engine, but then you have to complicate things because the 'drive train' is more like a model of the Beijing Anomaly."

"Which is what?"

"Oh, I just guessed Michael would have mentioned that casually at dinner or something."

"No."

"Some of the best acoustic testing in the world has been done on the lithosphere under China, they get readings that say that there is an ocean under the mantle that is as large as the Arctic ocean. They can tell it is saltwater. If that weren't surprising enough, there is the question of how it interfaces with the magma core. I hope you are having a good day, because nothing makes me feel more tenuous than talking about whole continents that are simply bridged above vast submantle oceans as though they just landed there..."

Elana chuckled. "Wow."

"So...the simulation is taking the bits of accounts that say something—anything--about catastrophic changes to the mantle. Now, in Genesis that's the breaking up of the 'fountains of the great deep.'

"People have the impression that Genesis is a quaint little story about heavy rain. But we know enough about it now to realize there is quite a different scene in mind. He meant volcanic magma or high-pressure water blown out from that or both. It never vaporized; it just fell from being sprayed out in all directions, and swelling up from below.

"But the thing about the term 'the deep' is that it is in the title of the collection of the oldest Babylonian materials too. SHA NAQBA IMURU means 'He who saw the deep.' He saw these things happen, but he also was suffering some, errr, sexual rejection. That is, Gilgamesh's friend was in trouble with a goddess for not accepting her attempt to seduce him, and he was killed.

"What in the world?" cried Elana. "It sounds like an archtype or something."

"So Gilgamesh is on a quest for eternal life, but comes to a miserable conclusion through Utnapushtim, which is the character in the story like Noah, who tells him it can't be obtained. That's because it was only found in a plant now at the bottom of Bahrain Bay in the Persian Gulf, and it is gone—out of reach. It's not a perfect match of Genesis 1-11, but many of the working parts are there—that one would be the 'tree of life' that can't be reached by mankind.

"Now, in the Chinese Shang-Ti, it opens by saying 'the earth was without form and dark' which would remind anyone of Genesis 1's opening stage, but they might not know that things develop from there."

"Develop?"

"The land appears—God makes the land appear and it is said to be 'on' the deep. There isn't any rain but there is a mist that comes from the deep. That is, there isn't any rain until the flood, and that's when we hear about the deep again. The fountains of the deep break open.

"The deep breaks open and then next thing we know is that there is a deluge and rain everywhere for half a year. A massive and catastrophic climate change. We know from a few other Biblical passages and from other materials that the fountains of the deep and the foundations of the earth (which usually meant the mantle) were known features and entities to ancient people. We know from other accounts and evidence that they actually knew quite a bit more about what was going on than we in our high-tech age *want* to think they knew.

"So the simulation takes these pieces and replicates the physical movement of them in a global catastrophe. We have incorporated plate tectonics because Genesis 1 mentions the forming of one landmass unit. The waters or deep are everywhere at first, and then they are 'gathered to one place' so that dry ground can appear. It's very likely that it's Genesis way of referring to 'Pangaea'—where everything is one piece. The sea is also one unit—the 'Epeiric.' Then when the deluge comes is the next time anything happens to this one landmass and one ocean.

"There is a person named Peleg in the Genesis account born right after the flood and his name means *division*, in reference to the earth. He lived when this happened twice actually. Once is the event mentioned so far—the deluge, or tectonic activity due to it. We find that the world is now divided that way or being divided. We also find that it is being divided linguistically or culturally.

"So now we have all these languages and places all over earth in more isolation than ever. And the interesting thing about that is that now, in modern times, we have the study of *geo-mythology*—the connection between geology and legend. Adrienne Mayor down at Stanford. And guess what topic came up first in the beginning of this area of study? A world deluge, because the 'first fossil hunters' as Mayor called them, were trying to explain to their descendants how it was that *ocean shells and marine fossils ended up inland and on mountains—all over the world.*"

"So your simulation shows the geologic motion you've just mentioned?"

"Yes, and any related hydrological or seismic activity we think was part of this. We call it catastrophic plate tectonics, CPT."

"I'll ask Michael. I don't think he's ever mentioned it. But I'd love to see it. I think my son would, too. He's not real crazy about learning about slow, murky water settling for millions of years."

"It has a way of dead-ending," Cam continued, "if you'll pardon the pun, because it is a story of God's destruction of a whole world that was called wicked, and which is also called violent. That's not everyone's favorite memory to rerun, you know. In Plato's *Timaeus* he says the gods made the flood happen because of all the fighting. Out on the Olympic Peninsula, the S'Klallam say that a slide came down to separate some ancestors who were continually fighting in one valley, and they lived apart ever after that.

"The orthodox university geologist just has one 'non-conforming' event, that I know of. An asteroid strikes the earth, close enough to what is now north America to spray metal particles all around. The dinosaurs die. Underground mammals survive. So they say. I have my doubts, but at least there is an exception. It's odd how they will allow that one, but never 'in a million years' look at what rapid sediment shows."

"So what does all that have to do with our missing carving?"

"Oh, that's just general information about flooding... What is difficult to get use to is how much material can be transported and how far. It reminds me of the old Volvo 200 series use of momentum. They were heavy tanks you know, to reach the safety goals they wanted. But they also knew that when something that heavy gets up to speed then miles per gallon goes up and it can range a long ways. I know one with 350K miles and it gets 37 out on the highway.

"Well, these floods and slurries of material, if you get them up to speed, can really push out the distance. So when we're out looking for something like your elk carving, we have to keep in mind how high the flood was at that point. What speed indications there are. How far had it traveled that high, etc. I'm loving it because it sharpens the science on both sides— both this investigation and catastrophes in general. Micro and macro. I get to solve a mystery, maybe a crime, but I also get to try out some formulas on mass movement. Now, you know what Monument Valley looks like, right?"

"Yeah, New Mexico. Four Corners."

"But I mean, how would you describe what you see there?"

"Errr, columns, or towers. Standing alone many times. Buttes."

"Good, good. I'm going to say it in a way that hopefully sharpens it. All of what you see is the *reciprocal* of what happened."

"Reciprocal?"

"The stand-alone rock columns and towers—they are what's *left*. But what happened? What happened is that walls of slurry flew through there and scoured out everything else! Monument? Yes! It's a *monument to the deluge!* We're talking about gigantic forces throwing their weight around; sandstone from New England ends up in Arizona! A slurry of marine nautiloids from the bottom of the ocean runs 150 miles from Grand Canyon to Las Vegas! The entire center of Australia is a rapid-deposit sediment. The entire center! That's huge. What kind of force—what size bulldozer—does it take to move material like that? To bend Ayers Rock into the shape of a J with all of its 'poorly-sorted' jagged granite. Or look at the *opisthotonic* postures— those dinosaurs you see plastered helplessly against some wall or rock. Death by natural causes? Nope. By a predator? Not a chance. They are usually intact. That's the thinking now from the geologists. Do you see?"

"Yeah, I doubt an elk carving could manage to make it through an event like we've had."

"Don't even think about it. It's just something to keep an eye out for. I'll be sifting through other channels first because there is so much physical work involved in trying to locate something like this. We'll let all the contractors do what they need to first and see if anything pops up from all the cleanup. That's at least three months."

"Other channels?"

"I'm a detective, right? I can't tell you about them or I'd have to shoot you, ha, ha!"

Elana chuckles. "You know your stuff."

"Come to one of my presentations."

"How's that?"

"Presentations on CPT. Bring Will. Do you know those Twitter feed maps?"

"Hmmm, not really."

"During an incident or a key piece of news, you can look on a Twitter feed map and find a geographic placement for various topics. Let's say Paris is attacked. Obviously Paris will be abuzz with tweets. So that's not interesting. What's interesting is to find out where else. But when a certain story has a particular impact on a certain place, then the map swells. Let's say Obama talks about the California drought. The Central Valley goes boom on Twitter.

"Now let's talk about geo-mythology. If a fairly coherent story about a family, sometimes referred to as specific as a family of 8, sometimes referred to as surviving in a huge ship, is found all over the planet from ancient times, then you can map out the specificity. You make a small circle when there are only a few common details. When it is large there are lots of common details. One part of our CPT video will be showing this. Our friends who think this flood was local—Mediterranean or Mesopotamian—will be surprised to see where some of the large circles show up. It will look like an ancient Twitter-feed map."

"So do you think there's a chance?"

"That the Genesis flood is reality-based?"

"No. The elk. Do you think we'll find it?"

"Can't make any promises. I definitely think a person will make themselves miserable trying."

41

"Yeah, good advice."

"What about reality-based, though?"

"*Genesis?*"

"Yeah."

Elana was silent for a moment. Cam waited. "You know, the thing that bothers me about people who have certain beliefs is when they start telling those who differ with them that the differing belief is not allowed."

"I apologize. I didn't realize..."

"Not you. *Michael!* He does that about his geology, and he's got his mind made up that the elk is nearby in the muck and you're not allowed to think any other way about it."

"But I *do.*"

"I know, I know. That's the point. He's a..., he's just got to have control, he's used to having control of people for decades now at his department, he's a 'sheriff' in the world of 'thought police'..."

Cam was glad inwardly to hear Elana sort things out. But he grieved for Michael and all the generations controlled by evolutionary humanists. "Elana, I need to get going here, could I give you Shara's number—the animator?"

"Sure, sure. Talk to you soon."

~ ~ ~

Cam invited Michael and Elana to the Great Southwest Restaurant off I-5 for a talk. The Monument Valley images were beautifully rendered on a HD mural in a room where they meet. When Michael and Elana came in, Cam was at the opposite wall of the room, studying the huge picture for any patterns he may have missed in previous looks.

"I'm just wishing I was just hovering above this place, up in the air over it and checking for patterns in it. But how are you today?"

"Just wondering why this is so slow."

"But certainly you understand there are some priorities which govern our work. If there's children involved, if there's domestic violence, if there's a homicide, we have to..."

"I've hired an excavator. He's going to poke around a bit wherever the access allows."

"I see... Well, good luck with that. And who did you hire, by the way?"

Michael checked for a card in his wallet. "Excel-Land. When he answers the phone, he says it fast and you think he said 'Excellent.'"

"And you're familiar with what goes on out there in one of these storms? I'd like to give you just a glimpse. You see, there seems to be a layering that slants up because the force of the river is pushing so much

42

material through at first, then less forcefully. So the next next layers come and slant back toward the river, in each given pile. That's why you see it punch things out of existing mounds and so on."

He pointed over at one section of Monument Valley. "Now just imagine one of those sloshing along and punching through what was Monument Valley and ending up on the Colorado Plateau at Grand Canyon."

But he stopped there to see what wheels would turn in Michael's mind. Cam sat fixed on the mural. Elana looked at him. Then she looked at Michael. Michael stared silently, perplexed. He glanced at Cam. He returned to the mural. Something huge was stirring in him, because something huge was forming in his understanding of the shapes of Monument Valley.

It was something like that optical illusion illustration of the two lamps. Or at least you think you see two lamps but then you see a silhouette of a face. He looked again at Monument Valley and envisioned the blitz, the fury, of stormy, icy sediment blasting through there, instead of the baked rocks out there now in 100' F weather. His elbow drifted off the table and he had to catch himself and his thoughts were interrupted.

Cam brought them back to the missing elk. "But what if the excavator wants to go out in the channel? I doubt if he can—without violating some kind of code. Is he desparate for money?"

"I don't know. That's his job to find out about access."

"Cam. I want to ask you something about 'geo-mythology,'" interjected Elana.

Cam glanced at each of them a little wary. "*Do* you?" he responded as though she needed to be careful.

"Geo-*what?*" asked Michael, shaking his head.

"Maybe another time, OK?" said Cam, solving that issue. "So if it was me Michael, I'd be hiking around all the pile-ups near you and looking on top, because the dry floating objects tend to end up there, and the bursts of energy in the floods put them up high."

4

MISACCUSATIONS

It had been a month since the deluge now, and Cam's suspicions and knowledge of criminal psychology had led him to consider how the theft and 'marketing' of the Ostrand carving might have happened. He was systematically checking the counties around the northwest that were prosperous enough to have people plunking down several thousand dollars on unusual landscape artwork advertised online. In this context, "Northwest" meant the Bay Area and north. And Salt Lake City and northwest. You had to think in terms of what the LA market would call "northwest" to keep up with these guys. He was looking through listings of building permits.

He tended toward Marin County partly because of the Redwoods nearby. And because of the enforcement of building permit records about items such as this. He found an elk. How many elk carvings would be sold under "landscape art" in that time period? He felt a step closer.

He now consulted with the sheriff on producing a notice to the Snohomish public about any suspicious activity in the area of the Ostrand-Morton place. The sheriff decided to go for it if Michael would match their own in-house notices with some of his own in the newspapers and around town. He was a bit exasperated. "We've got so many other things to look into!"

Amanda Reese was on shift the day at the Zip-In-Out convenience store when Michael came in with his poster for information wanted. Amanda was bored and read the notice immediately to perk herself up. She didn't need any more coffee at that point. The notice would do just fine. She and Michael had a short conversation and Michael called Cam.

~ ~ ~

Cam had given Shara's details to Elana. Shara worked from home. She'd gone into graphics from her university days when she knew Cam. She found an opportunity in LA in high profile CGA work and got up to speed, but "LA—sheesh, you couldn't pay me to live there!" which was a rather precise description of what was happening economically. The middle class had

45

disappeared and an understanding of the disappearance of the middle class had disappeared. You either did or did not 'get paid' to live there; you had either made it or you got public assistance.

Elana found the office door at Shara's and stepped in.

"Oh, hi. I'm...not exactly a customer, but you are who I was trying to reach. I'm Elana. Elana Morton, and I'm Michael Ostrand's wife—partner, really." She sighed. "Anyway, I've been talking to Cam...Cam Berra, the detective..."

Shara made a note of the sigh and the 'anyway' for later. "Yes, yes, go ahead."

"I'm not trying to meddle with a case or anything, I was just interested in hearing more about the CPT DVD without bothering him."

"Yeah, interesting guy. I moved back from LA because I just couldn't see living in that world day in and day out, and no seasons, it seems. But he—he was happily in the geology program at UW until they found out he was more suspicious; he was actually a detective who happened to be working in geology."

"How so you mean?"

"Well, he was reading C. S. Lewis about the naturalist or uniformitarian scientists when he realized it was all set up wrong."

"What was wrong? You're not being clear."

"The science." Shara reached for a book that was handy to her library. GOD IN THE DOCK. She slid it across the desk to Elana, who sat across from her to absorb this. "It's a British expression; it means God on trial."

Elana put 2 and 2 together and asks: "So is God being 'accused' of a 'crime'?"

Shara laughed slightly. "Well, it's curious that you should ask the question that way. No, only of a twist from the—let's say—*predictable*. What the scientists would call 'conforming'."

"I don't get it."

"It means 'God on trial—on the stand.' So, yeah, it's sort of the idea that God has committed some 'crime,' and people have summoned Him to answer."

"Ahhh, yes, well that's about as much as I know about Him. 'Where is God when...?' Everyone I know sort of stops there. And gives up."

"Right. Let's come back to that, but this 'crime' is to differ with the scientists—especially the geologists—who flooded the world with uniformitarianism."

Shara was speaking as though uniformitarianism was a sort of nerve gas while the rest of the culture paid no more attention to it than it did to air. "First I'll tell you a bit more about Cam. You see, he was at the U back in the 90s, and he was really interested in geology."

"I wonder if he and Michael met there."

"I don't know, but there was a catch. He was already reading heavily about *catastrophism* and he wanted to pursue that."

"Do you mean Velikovsky and comets and asteroids and all that?"

"Well, not exactly. Because to study that you'd have to work on astronomy and astrophysics. I'm sure he looked into it a bit. But in science, he's 'down to *earth*'--so to speak."

"That's the leading view of why the dinosaurs are gone, I think—asteroids."

"He was more about finding things in the stratigraphy that were anomalies or non-conforming or otherwise just didn't make sense. Cam decided there was so much non-conforming that it didn't make any sense to have the category! So he was chased out of geology at the UW."

"Hmmm, the 90s?"

"So, maybe they knew each other. Well, anyway, they told him not to pursue that line of interest. And that struck him as odd...because I think there was more detective in him than he realized. Let me read you how the Lewis conversation goes with the uniformitarian. You know who I mean?"

"Well, I know who Lewis was. NARNIA and all that."

"Yeah, Oxford literature chair. In the 30s, 40s. Pals with Tolkien, etc. No stranger personally to the question of 'where is God?' either, but he seems to have been balanced enough to realize that's only one question."

"'*Only* one question'?"

"Do you know the 'missing ceiling tile' syndrome?'"

"No, how do you mean?"

"It's a sort of psychology's oxygen saturation meter—you know those things the nurse has you put on your finger for a physical now that checks your blood's oxygen content?"

"Do I ever."

Shara put the book down. "How do *you* mean?"

"It's Darcy, my daughter. It's congenital I guess, but yeah, we already have to watch hypoxemia. *Under*--too *little* oxygen. Hard to go to the mountain tops, etc."

"Oh, the poor thing. I'd like to meet her some time. So what happens? Are there panic attacks? And you were on your own that night during the crest of the Snohomish, weren't you?"

Elana tensed up as she remembered the night, but she welcomed the attention from Shara. She teared for a moment. "You're...you really care, don't you? Thanks. It's just that... There's all that driving Darcy around with her feet out the window..."

Shara looked in close on Elana. Elana was collapsing at her desk. Shara pulled up a chair around beside her.

"Well, can you not tell anyone this?"

Shara reached to rub her back. The conversation was now quiet as there was something big on Elana's heart. "Is it OK?" Shara asked, indicating her arm about to stroke Elana across the back.

Elana melted a bit more and nodded. "I really *was* frightened. It was just so dark and chaotic, although I knew we were up a ways above high water marks and all that in our house, but still, when its just you and the kids, and you just imagine the vulnerable miles between you and your partner. Actually, I was afraid our lane had been wiped out.

"I woke up in a sweat, a nightmare. I scared Darcy—she said I was yelling. I guess it was instinctive. The connection by car to others and things you need seemed so vital. I didn't mention a thing to Will—well, he thinks like a boy that it's all cool to see things get destroyed and wild, and I had to keep him down at the other end of the house."

"The miles?"

"You just think about I-5 and how nothing could ever happen there, but then when you live out here in the woods, there's so many little roads and places and weird things that can happen. I had a friend once in some flooding in Oregon, south of Portland. He was a brilliant special education teacher but he had a weak heart, and he was out driving, and all of a sudden he was stuck, or landlocked or something. I don't know exactly, but he couldn't get back and he had a heart issue, I mean, an episode, and it happened out there and he didn't make it."

Shara leaned in. "And you thought the worst might happen to Darcy that night?"

"Well, yeah, but it's something else..."

"I promise. *No one.* I won't talk."

"Well, it's just that Michael came home the next afternoon. I mean it was that long before they let people drive our road, and it had been almost 24 hours and we had phone contact, and maybe that's all he thought I needed, but he never came to the house. He just got on the lane at the bottom and looked at the damage and the missing carving. He never even came to see me or Darcy first, he just went off back down the road and started looking."

"And you felt neglected like other times or was this new?"

"I called and he didn't answer. I guess the river noise was loud and all that, but still. It was a double dose... I think he was interested in the children when they were little, but I don't know if he's interested anymore. I mean Shara, you've kind of been missing, dead. Wouldn't you come and hug those who meant a lot to you? The prospect for Darcy is portable oxygen tanks and things and difficulty sleeping, and he's like 'what does this have to do with me?' But the odd thing is it's not really that big of a deal. I mean she's young and she can work up her physical strength. It's his inability to accept that

48

there is a defect that is more difficult to accept than the condition itself. He about flies off the handle when she says the H word, and her cycle hasn't even started. It's just an awful marriage."

"*Marriage?* I thought..."

"Did I say that?" Elana laughed humbly. Elana needed to unpack what had just happened. They were quiet. Shara kept her arm around Elana sympathetically.

"Yes, I think I know what you mean..." Shara finally continued, thinking that Elana had just made a 'hard landing' and couldn't recover from it. "Let me tell you about the syndrome—the missing ceiling tile?"

"Thank you for caring, Shara... So I have to ask you—are you just extra friendly or why do you care? Or are you—you know—actually seeking a woman partner...?"

Shara blushed embarrassed. "Ah, well that's a bit of the risk of care these days, isn't it? There's all those kinds of love out there and they seem to overlap. And now in our mass media, you'd get the idea that the only time two women would care about each other was because they want to be intimate. No, I have my children, too. But I'm a Christian, Elana, a follower of Christ, and I hope that my 'brand' or 'mark' is love—or care."

"I see. Right. OK, well, what's the syndrome?"

"It's about what a person is like when they go into a meeting room or a classroom or office and are waiting, and they notice almost nothing about the room except that one ceiling tile or panel is missing. So I guess a classroom isn't the best example today because they are kind of run down! But it's just that fixation on the one 'mistake' or the thing missing. Or a woman can come into your room with perfect legs and all you do is worry about your, you know, extra pounds."

"What made you think of that?"

"I don't remember!" Shara laughs disarmingly. She stares about her office, trying to retrieve their conversation and how that came up. She looks at the book by Lewis. "It'll come back. Now, let's see, where was that conversation Lewis was having?... It will come. "Religion and Science" is the name of... OK, here:

"Miracles," said my friend, "Oh, come. Science has knocked the bottom out of all that. We know that Nature is governed by fixed laws."

"But, don't you see," said I, "that science never could show that anything [was beyond Nature]?"

51

"Why on earth not?"

"Because science studies Nature. And the question is whether anything <u>besides</u> Nature exists—anything "outside." How could you find that out by

49

studying simply Nature?'

"Look here," he said "Could this 'something outside' that you talk about make two and two five?"

"Well, no," said I.

"All right. The idea of their being altered is as absurd as the idea of altering the laws of math."

"Half a moment. Suppose you put a nickel into a drawer today and another in the same drawer tomorrow. You plan to do that each day from now on. Do the laws of arithmetic make it certain that you'll find 15 cents there the next day?"

"Of course, provided no one's been tampering with your drawer."

"Ah, but that's the whole point," I said. "The laws of arithmetic can tell you what you'll find, with absolute certainty, provided that there's no interference. If a thief has been at the drawer of course you'll get a different result. But the thief won't have broken the laws of math—only the laws of the land. Now, aren't the laws of Nature much in the same boat? Don't they all tell you what will happen provided there's no interference?...The laws will tell you how a billiard ball will travel on a smooth surface if you hit it in a particular way—but only provided no one interferes. If they do, you won't get what the scientist predicted."

"No, of course not. He can't allow for monkey tricks like that."

"Quite. And in the same way, if there was anything outside Nature, and if it interfered—then the events which the scientist expected wouldn't follow. That would be what we call a <u>miracle</u>. In one sense it wouldn't break the laws of Nature...But they can't tell you if something is going to interfere. I mean, it is not the expert at math who can tell you how likely someone is to interfere with the pennies in my drawer. A detective, or a psychologist, or a metaphysician would be better."

"So Cam found that line by Lewis at that time in his life, and that's when he realized 'I'm actually a *detective* who wanted to work in geology.' It'll have to be a hobby while I make a career in forensics."

"But Shara, you don't strike me as being one of those people who are having miracles happen all the time or at least think they are—until you find out later that they really weren't all that impossible."

"And they butt heads with the atheists who say it *can't* happen," added Shara, "And those two kind of feed off of each other's denial of each other in a never-ending contest of wills."

"Right. But you're not that way, I don't think. You're real. You'd never be trying to be on TV on those goofy Christian shows, or building a full-scale ark in the Bible belt as though just constructing one somehow proved the whole thing true."

50

"I think it would be a huge mistake to tell people when God is going to do a miracle, but I would not rule it out like the scientist—like in the conversation. And this uniformitarian stuff—it's just so sterile, so lifeless. You listen to Cam for a while and you realize there's been lots of forceful things happening very quickly. It's totally different."

The women turned quiet and finally Elana took stock. "There's a lot to think about."

"I know, and I really haven't told you that much about what Cam and I are working on!"

"Can I ask you something else, though?"

"Sure. Then maybe I can get our simulation running for you."

"He's not your husband, right?"

"No, just friends from school and college, and church and this project is a bit of a church and a professional contact."

"And that's OK with your husband?"

"It's all out in the open. No one's in bed with someone else's partner. I'd stop dealing with him if I thought that. We have a solid church that respects marriage vows taken by its members. We all believe that's the only place for sex—and that marriages belong in a 'network' where members respect the marriages."

"Oh." When she heard that, Elana had a glimpse of how destroyed society actually was; it was as though it was her first view over an edge of the Grand Canyon and there was nothing, nothing for 3000 feet, and she gasped someplace so deep inside her she had no name for it. "And so...what about those other kinds of love you just talked about?"

"Oh, serial sexual partners aren't in love. They may look like it, but that's not really what's going on inside, is it? Sex is—what do they say?—only 2% of a relationship, in the same sense that words are only 25% of communication, or so. But everyone is *told* by a deluge of media, by Hollywood, that that 2% has two 0s behind it, and so we have all the kinds of sexual confusion which they have created. And all these sexually-confused people in this sexual socialist state are being told that they have irrefutable sexual rights from the government for anything they desire, even teen-agers. They find these rights dripping right from the Constitution—like that's why the country was started! Lewis had an brilliant expression about this. He said they were 'sacrificing their consciences on the altar of eros.'

"There's a book out there called GETTING TO NO SEX, and it's by a Christian counselor, and what she meant was to clarify all this—that there is no reason at all why a caring relationship has to go sex-ward—to go that direction. So, you might say, Christians are really free because they are not trying to make anything happen along that line; that *virtues* really are higher and uplifting and inspiring: honesty, trust, compassion, endurance. That's

51

because our Savior said 'The truth will set you free.'

"Do you remember the line from Tolstoy in *ANNA KARENINA?* She had called it right about her brother's indiscretion with a governess, and then his remorse.

That's shameful, disgraceful, but it was not love. That was the animal in man, not the soul. Stiva's remorse is from the soul...

You can't neglect your soul."

Elana nodded. "We read that, once, in college. That's as close as I got to believing in a soul, or at least that there must be two parts to us...in conflict... You know what? I think I'll get back to you about Cam. I mean about the simulation video. I've taken in about all I can and I should check on Darcy."

"Well, to be honest, this project is really a better thing to see down at Delta anyway."

"What'sthat?"

"It's a digital service with huge capacity servers and processors. When you want to finish out something in HD digital, it's way too expensive for the average graphics designer or animator, so you just go down there and rent some lab time. We'll go some time, OK? Just you and me. And we'll talk more. About driving around with Darcy's feet hanging out."

"Yeah, thanks."

~ ~ ~

Martin was riveted to the bulletin board outside the Zip-In-Out, when he was startled and dropped his 6-pack of Blue Moon Apple Ale. 4 of them broke all over the sidewalk. He was looking at a notice for information about suspicious activity in the 2700 block area along the river the night after it peaked in November. The notice was from BlueTeeth Security, a private investigative company. "Two won't handle it! I gotta go back."

He went back inside to buy another, and went to the other till so as not to bring up the topic of spilt beer out in front. Amanda was at the other till and detached from the TV as he came to pay. She'd been listening to local reports.

"You know that big elk carving up there along the Snoho? Now they're saying it might not have been just the river pounding away during that flood. They are asking for information about it."

"Oh? I don't know anything about that."

She wasn't sure exactly why, but she didn't believe him.

~ ~ ~

Jeff had been parked at the Zip and noticed Martin. He thought Martin had become increasingly unsettled, then he saw him drop his beer in front of the notice board. In fact, he just watched Martin this time, and Martin didn't even notice Jeff's pickup when he walked by, which he normally would. Martin was drowning in whatever it was that absorbed him.

After Martin was gone, Jeff went over and checked out the board himself. There was the notice about the missing carving.

A deluge of suspicion came over him. He'd better start looking for some other place to work. There was too much about Martin he didn't know.

~ ~ ~

Cam reached a deputy in Marin County and emailed down several documents. The deputy called back the next day. Found.

"The owner's in shock. Pretty sure he had no idea what was going on, but here's something to work on."

"What's that?"

"The antlers are real, as you may have noticed, but one of the points is broken. It's a fresh break for sure. R3. I don't know how this thing got here, but there's the question of whether the break happened in transit or back in S...n...o...--what's that?"

"*Snohomish* County. And river. It's been missing since a major flood in November."

"If you haven't asked the public for help, now's the time. That would be a huge piece of confirmation. And then there's the girl."

"The girl?"

"There's a missing person report, the same week, and last seen is the same address."

"What's this about? Where? I never heard a thing. I mean, where is the listing? The Boss will really jump into this now."

~ ~ ~

Through Amanda's tip—or really the tip of her mother who just happened to be curious about the "late shift" down on their road—Cam had a new tactic.

He had paid a visit to the road department scheduler about activity that night and learned that the emergency crews had done nothing in the area on those days. Some type of crew had been out there but it was not one of the official crews.

He then explained to Michael that the sheriff's office had equipment operators over in the road department he could draw upon for a little 'gold

53

panning'--which meant fine sifting for evidence. And he now had a warrant for treating the area Amanda mentioned as a crime scene. He understood Michael had hired an excavator but he wouldn't be needed, as there was now an arrangement for the sifting. Within hours, an area near the mail boxes was taped off with the familiar yellow boundary crime scene tape. Some extra lighting was brought in. Cam would check in frequently.

The process was simple. The road crew would retrieve several soil samples right here. Loads of mud would be put on the jiggling, screening platform and a portable water pump would be set up to spray out the screen to see if anything unusual emerged from that location.

Martin had a reckless sense of curiosity and was driving along the area one of these afternoons. He became alarmed as he saw an unmarked but official vehicle parked in the area and the boundary tape. He drove past and returned and came back to where he could watch in his rear view mirror.

As Cam was making notes, he noticed that Martin's pickup had parked. It was Excel-land Excavating. Cam made a note and checked the local business listings.

~ ~ ~

"So Elana. You know what a Twitter map is, right?" Shara and Elana sat at the lab desk at Delta with its window facing out to a screening room's large screen.

"I know what Twitter is. Not the map."

"It is a geographic representation of how much a topic is being discussed in a geographic area. I guess Twitter can anonymously eavesdrop and search twitters and score how much a topic is being discussed and where. Now, that doesn't seem to have much to do with Cam and his topic."

"Right."

"So...have a look at this." At Delta Studios, she could exhibit the latest workup of a project on a huge screen, for which several technicians waited their turn. There were three booths at work, but only one at a time could use the large screen feature for up to 3 minutes at a time, at which point it was the next booths turn. The booths could not see the others or the others work, either. The same facility was used for private party screenings a few times each week.

"Instead of Twitter symbols, Cam had me put a tsunami wave logo at various points around the ancient world. So this is the whole ancient world, showing the continent of Pangaea, which, up to the point of the Genesis deluge does not conflict with what Genesis says. The size of the logo corresponds, through his conclusions, to the amount of impact the deluge account seems to have had—how deeply held by a culture. At that point it is

54

not as objective as a Twitter map."

The segment started into motion with the large dots in Greece, Egypt, Babylonia, Scandinavia, India. It also began with a 'pangaea' world of one continent. Then the continental lines emerged, the continent shapes became defined, and the dots began to disperse into smaller ones, so that the total *coverage volume* of them remained the same, but there were many, many more of them until it spread with all the continents and amounted to hundreds.

"It's like 500, more or less. All around the world."

"And this is essentially both Biblically and anthropologically sound?" Elana was intrigued and impressed.

"If anything, the deluge was too narrow as a topic to mark. He could have gone with other topics. But it clarified the animated image to have it just dwell on one. Genesis 1-11 is rather rich in topics and moves very easily between them as topics go. But yes, it's what Mayor was speaking of and James-Griffith. These themes are found throughout these places, but always a bit dented or cracked, like pottery that had to make a long trek on the back of a donkey on a rocky road."

"Shara, what happened?—I mean in England in the 1800s when all these people pop up teaching these completely-worked out alternatives to and rejections of such well-demonstrated knowledge?"

"I don't know. Ask Cam. I just know that it was such a huge shift when the president of Harvard appointed a new law department chief, Dr. Langdell, because he not only had replaced the Bible with ORIGIN OF SPECIES, he replaced the *language*, the expressions. Law now *evolved, mutated, generated*. I think Lyell was way over his head, and was making declarations that were way beyond what he really knew to be true. They—Lyell, Thomas Huxley, etc.--simply wanted to 'end' Christianity. Subscribing only to 'processes we can see' sounds good, but there's a history of some very fast-moving turbulence out there, and he would lose his grip on all that right off."

~ ~ ~

Jeff was working on his pickup one day and he had to reset all his radio settings after undoing the battery. Actually, he was always working on the thing, and always pretending to impress Stacey with the fact that he had wheels. But now there was no Stacey. He chanced on some local news just as a sentence was ending "...*the carving has been missing since the major Snohomish flood earlier this winter...*"

It made him stop what he was doing. He missed Stacey and wondered what happened to her on that trip. But he wasn't active about it. He didn't really know who to talk to and he didn't want to run into some awful news.

He left it alone. He thought about that last conversation they had when she was daydreaming about motherhood. Or at least that's what it sounded like to him.

The last sentence on the radio also made him pushed to do something he didn't want to be bothered with. What if they were talking about Martin's elk, and was that the police asking or just the owner? And where was he? Maybe he needed to cut it off with Martin. But he knew how much fun it would be looking for work right now. He sighed.

~ ~ ~

Elana was having trouble keeping away from a small stack of books she had collected. And then there were all those speakers on youtube. As far as Elana was concerned, those English thinkers had pretended an ancient past world and tried to create a new one based on that pretending. Badly done, considering violent rivers that rumble occasionally with only a hundredth of what of what they could work up. Not to mention the oceans, and volcanoes. There were all kinds of ways this was so unsatisfactory in geology. How exactly, like the scientist from Australia said, do you put 6000 feet of sediment on top of a mile of bedrock and push the whole thing up a mile--quickly? Or even 6 feet! And then there were all the legends and accounts from hundreds of tribes and ancient peoples. She knew how important they were to each one, even locally. How could a person ever come to a coherent cosmology?

Elana was starting to see that Lyell made way too many announcements way before he really knew anything. That's what a whole century of "science" was like. Lyell had written to a friend that if he could just write up his theory about geology, he could "bury" Christianity. 'It's the problem of the *physico-theologians*' he had said. 'We've got to get rid of them.' That meant those theologians who believed Genesis 1-11 should be set right along side other reliable data about what happened in earth history. And so the minds of students of this century were crushed under the layers of oversimplifications of Lyell's personal desires.

He was not one to physically harm anyone. Out of the question. But invent an explanation of stratigraphy that rendered Genesis irrelevant? Absolutely.

Among the 'other reliable data' was a report coming from 'the end of the earth'--Naszca, Peru. In 1570, a Spanish priest had visited that 14,000 foot altitude village and found a whole mountain of incredible indications—or not so incredible. He mentioned thousands of sacred burial stones in which humans were shown with dinosaurs, both in conflict, and riding them; accounts of a one true creator Viracocha, from whom several people through the generations had departed for the worship of animals and beasts;

Viracocha prohibited images of himself. He continued with indications of very technically-advanced people who had hot air balloons from which to make their huge stone diagrams; details about insects in the diagrams which could not have been made unless people worked with microscopes; people who could cut, transport, and lay granite from a hundred miles away into stone walls that appeared to know the latest in protection from earthquakes by using irregular rather than mass-produced layouts and which used poured-metal staples for some connections; a huge number of stones depicting savage killing as something to memorialize, along with a large number of bizarre sexual images; accounts of that Creator also sending a flood because of the evil of the world, because they were brainless giants without any morals; accounts that that Creator would *not* flood the world again but instead had a son who would come and give his life for the offense of the world against the Creator; an account of a person name 'Tomas' with his tablets of truth which confirmed all of the above; a belief that a meal of wine and bread were to be taken in memory of that son.

None of which would fit easily, if at all, into the mind of Lyell, Huxley and Darwin as they spread their mythology around the world. William Wilberforce had struck a blow for Christianity against the superiority of the British empire. It was coming apart. It was coming apart in the American Revolution with its documents rooted in a direct connection between citizen and Creator. *Creator!* That was it! All they had to do was undermine the Creator, and their Imperial racism would win back the world from the 'horror' of what was going on over in America. Make Him out as hallucination, or madness, or fantasy, or primitive legend—anything but the everlasting Creator, Redeemer and Judge of the Christians.

That racism element was what was really going on there. Darwin had said so right from the title page of the originals of ORIGINS—that *the fittest races should win in their struggle.* None of this 'endowed by a Creator with rights' poppycock concocted by the Americans! It was Darwin who wrote:

At some future period, not very distant as measured by centuries, the civilized races of man will almost certainly exterminate, and replace, the savage races throughout the world.

That was why Jane Austen's MANSFIELD PARK was a double shock. Here were the fabulous mansions of England financed by the horrible machine of slavery and sugar, and the Christians were opposing it. But who or what was entirely comfortable with the 'struggle' to 'evolve'? The *landed class,* now comforted even more by Huxley's and Lyell's fantasy sciences. The same classes had believed rubbish about the native peoples where the empire spread. Austen knifed the ruling class in this exchange:

Mr. Bertram: But you know, strangely, the Tumulatas can never have children. They are like mules in that respect.

Edmund: Excuse me father, for contradicting you, but that is nonsense. You cannot say such things.

That's what kind of lies truly drove that generation to welcome evolution.

The Mosleyites, the Friday Club and the British Black Shirts all had the support of upper classes to peacefully *join* the Third Reich when it came, not fight it. *"This is not our war."* There were very advanced preparations, with contacts in Whitehall, and the House of Lords. The superior race would 'struggle together to win,' empowered by evolution, not preserving rights endowed by a Creator.

Or again, the Leftist revolution in American in the 1970s generation would claim America to be such a foul racist state. Yet it was formed to stop slavery by no less than Jefferson himself, basing itself on a Creator rather than an evolved State, which had the upper British class hopping mad. Or, in Jefferson's case, on an ethically reasonable Jesus. The Left was all misinformation and misaccusation about origins and outcomes, some of it shear hypocrisy, because the Left's social policies ruined African-Americans generally, making them fatherless victims generally, and the women victims of black men, entitled to so many welfare dollars per fatherless child. "Fair" outcomes versus fair opportunity.

Darwin personally had nothing against a belief system that had produced his lovely, caring wife. Nor its answer to death in the resurrection of Christ for the believer, when he believed he was see his dear daughter Annie again. Or would he, if he gave it up? But the 'friends' had their Imperial, racist victory to pursue. And some personal moral struggles, too. And he didn't have any other friends. They could be really nasty if you differed with them.

To win, they had to pound the public with their fantasy evidence of millions of years. After all, evolution had been proposed before, but only Hutton and Lyell seemed to realize that geological stratigraphy had to be rewritten to support millions of years.

The worst day in modern science was the day the BEAGLE tied up at the Rio Santa Cruz at the bottom of Argentina. It was not just bad because Darwin was seriously devouring Lyell's PRINCIPLES, but because he was devouring PRINCIPLES while his ship overlooked a glacial cut that could not possibly have happened over a million years. Or 6000 million. If he had just contemplated the reality in front of him instead of a theory written 9000 miles away, dripping with its agenda, he might have noticed the actual hydrology of the place. But he didn't. That day, and quite possibly that act (or lack of) was the day modern science ceased and became religion.

The uniformitarians asked for and snapped up any information coming back from the American frontier where piles of bones of massive creatures were found, which they now believed 'proved' Lyell's reverse projections back into time. It didn't matter if soft tissues of these beasts were in the condition that mountain men would describe as 'overdried jerky.' They had 'found Time' and they would play with it til everything hummed smootly.

And then they would somehow bury the increasingly unpopular racism as time went on. They would bury the connection between such evolution and racism until it only showed in a few seldom-visited traces of the literature. They would champion 'equality' as a social cause with all the secular feel-good force they could muster. And, hey, why just make *races* equal? Why not all classes in massive, centralized states? And why not genders and all sexual activity, dictated onto the masses in the media and by legislation? Evolve! Evolve!

And villify. Ridicule! Insult! Hit the opposition with overwhelming force and especially the young people. Make them feel stupid for not 'belonging' to the masses who worshipped at the feet of ORIGINS and PRINCIPLES.

And so Elana realized that modern America, and perhaps the West, had become a construction of misaccusations. The freedom in the Constitution and in the Creator really was why America had been so good for so many people. And those accusing America of racism in the 2010s were 50 to 100 years late, and relied on flimsy material like *their own* verdict about Fergeson, jamming the airwaves with provocative photographic misaccusations months before due process. How neatly that covered up the real race superiority problem embedded in evolution, as well as the abject failure of a socialist state attempting to be 'father' for millions of minority households. Elana recalled a line from Yeats:

The best lack all conviction, while the worst
Are full of passionate intensity.

So said Yeats, but Elana was not going to fail her convictions!

Elana was catching the outlines of these thoughts. They were forming and holding. She read some of the books Shara and Cam had. Some answers were coming. A deluge of information was turning into a deluge of suspicions. She didn't know if God talking to her was part of the deal, but she had no other way to describe it. Not the silliness found in so many outlets of religion and cults, but necessary, rational, practical ideas from the Christian message.

~ ~ ~

Martin decided to make another slow pass by the county's crew, who were acting on behalf of the sheriff, and see what the process was. It was not a machine with which he was familiar. He should have been in an unmarked car, but he was losing his edge. He should have had on his curious customer face, parked, walked over and introduced himself and explained that he was merely keeping up to speed on new machinery in the industry, with a marked vehicle and all that. Instead, his street sense was being drained by drink and by guilt.

He drove by slowly again and realized no police cars were there at the moment, only the crew of two with the screener/agitator device and the spray of water from the river. They were dredging. They were 'panning for gold' but Martin didn't know what the gold was, nor to whom. All he knew was that it was exactly where he had 'stashed' the carving back during his storm clean-up.

He had become too simple to be clandestine.

Martin's slow drive by there that day alerted one of the crew. "I think that's the 3rd time I've seen that excavator come by, studying us. I wonder what that's about?"

"I was wondering what any of this was about until the piece showed up. Well, we're almost done."

"Excel-Land. I'll tell Cam."

5

DISCREDITATIONS

"Cam, I really don't think Michael will come."

"Yeah, I think you're right." Michael and Elana had been invited to dinner at Berra's with Shara and Jim. Cam and Patrice lived in the Lake Stevens area.

"We're in two worlds, Cam. He's in a professional world where I don't think he can even mention to anyone that he's seen your animation, let alone talk about it. I'm out here with the children... But I have a mind, you know. So I'm trying to get that selection by Peter down, you know, 3-2."

"Try 2 as in 2nd letter, and 3 as in 3rd chapter. Although compared to a novel, you wouldn't call them chapters!"

"Yeah, yeah. But I did read that 2nd one, and that's where I was going to start with my questions."

Cam thought about that and knew the subject was a pretty harsh declaration about some wild, permissive types in early Christian groups. It was not where he would have started. "OK, what caught your attention?"

"It's that place—the blackest darkness. Or places. It says some angels rebelled from God and were banished there."

"Yes, that's right. So there had been things happening before we get to the creation of earth."

"Yes, but that's just it. I went back and read Genesis and there it was."

"What?"

"It's black and dark. The earth was."

Wheels turned in Cam's mind. He had been a reader for years. He had learned, for example, that when Moses wrote, he often had a structure to a segment. But here was a 'disinterested party'--you might say—reading a Biblical passage, and they saw something entirely new to him.

That structure by Moses went something to this effect:

1, summary statement or title

2, pre-existing situation
3, new action
4, possible repeat summary statement

But now, as was often the case, a brand new mind, and a good one, had taken one look, and put 2 things together that, as far as he knew, had never been connected.

And it made sense as far as this structure template went:

1, God created heaven and earth (summary or title)
2, the earth was formless, void, dark
3, God forms the place into something where there are life systems, climate, biology, humans
4, it was very good

But the real question was what Elana's discovery meant.

"I'll be checking into that! In my experience with the Bible, there are what you might call 'corners.' You come around them and realize it was trying to say something else than what you thought or what you have been hearing. Very, very interesting." He was not trained in theology, but he'd been talking to some of his friends in the area that had formed a network of scientists who believed the Bible in its ordinary sense—that it wasn't something you 'decode' or that Genesis 1 was not a total metaphor for some other story— like Israel arriving in its promised land. Genesis 1 was the most unusual passage in the world when taken in the ordinary sense. Which it called for.

On one hand, it was far more advanced and coherent that the several legends around the world that most scholars, instead of writing it off, were busy working on which derived from the other. Some at the highest level had shown that the others fragmented from it. On the other hand, there was the talking snake, and the mysterious, paradisaical tree and its fruit.

"Anything else, then, Elana? What did you find in the 3rd section?"

"Well, that was...*really* modern-sounding, I thought. I was struck by the skeptics! So how would Peter know that people like that would come along—unless, of course, there's 'outside' help! They just sound like Michael's friends. I don't know how he'd feel if he found out there was a declaration that discredited them!"

"Good, good. Now there is something here I don't want you to miss. We are reading something from the 1st century; Peter's first thought wasn't about us now. So let's backtrack just a bit. He lives in Judaism. He was raised in it. It's 1st-century Judaism and the Gospel which are in conflict. He's writing to those Christians, Jews and Gentiles, who now live out of the area, and he's been moving about the area himself.

"Those skeptics are asking 'Where is the promised coming?' Now if you were a 1st century follower of Judaism, you are asking: 'where is the Messiah that is promised, you Christians?' This is not surprising, because the rejection of Christ happens two ways: one was the event itself; the other is the rejection of *what that event meant* a little later as the generation moved along. If any thing is clear, the Christians said that Jesus (the historic set of events of his life for the debt of our sins) was the Christ.

"The firey end of the world hadn't happened when Peter wrote this, but it would be the plight of the land of Israel. So that's Peter's answer to Judaism. So there is both a *picture* there in what happened to Israel, and there is the *declaration* for the whole world. God is delaying that firey day so that more will believe. There is a mission, you see. We are on a mission. Every person who becomes a Christian is on one, even if they don't realize it, simply by virtue of having a message that bursts into the world when it is expressed. God wants all to be saved from sin's debt and depart from its influence."

"*Debt?*"

"Our sins are an accumulated debt. That's what God's forgiveness is about. He doesn't want us crushed under the, well, deluge of debt."

"I remember now--'*forgive us our debts...*' Remember? VBS. I remember VBS. You must have been there. But it's not "BS", is it? I don't remember the next."

"'*As we forgive those in debt to us.*'"

"Oh. But that would be those who *believe* they are in debt to us."

"Yes."

"What's for dinner? I'm starved. It's aroma is attacking me from the kitchen."

"Well..." jested Shara. "We thought we'd have some *elkloaf*!"

Everyone snorted. Cam spilled his drink.

~ ~ ~

"Yes, we are close. I can't tell you how, or why, but we are very close. We just have to set up the meeting." Cam had called Michael in since there seemed to be no let-up in Michael's calls about what was happening.

"Well, that's better. I'm not hearing anything from the excavator."

"Right. Needle in a haystack. That is, if he can even get to the haystack with equipment."

"I guess so."

"Remind me again, who did you have out there?"

Michael searched his wallet. "Excel-Land Excavating. His name is Martin."

Inwardly, Cam whirled around when he heard that name, but on the outside, remained detached and professional. "Well, it's not too late to take information from him if he does come upon something."

"In one spot he found a lamp."

"A lamp?"

"An upright. Wooden. Like you'd put by your easy chair in your living room. Pretty beat up."

"So that's that. Now, on our other business. Have you had any more thoughts about my presentation about the deluge or CPT?"

"Not very much."

Cam smiled, having expected as much. "Had you ever heard anything like that?"

"You guys need to stick to your make-believe, allright? This is really dangerous stuff when you start crossing over."

"Crossing-over?"

"When you start saying anything like this actually happened."

"Why is that?"

"It just *is.*"

"Look, I'll give you my own phone number. I just want you to chew on that and call me if you find the reason you're after—this thing you say 'just is'."

"Why?"

"Because I'm curious about people, about how they decide to do things. You see, we've got this coherent account of the world we live in, and it echoes in all those others around the world although unclearly sometimes, but that same Genesis account also tells us not to tamper with evidence."

"There is no evidence."

"I meant about *our* affairs, about *crime*—like your elk."

"You are really unclear."

"Someone took advantage of the storm, Michael, and hauled off *your* elk and sold it for a bundle. It's called *looting.* I can't tell you the details yet, but there it is. That's the path we are chasing down, and we've nearly caught up to him. But I'm talking about 'don't make a false witness' in God's commands. It seems to me that that Genesis and 'Mr. Moses' actually have a lot to do with what's happened to *your* elk, and are very helpful, Michael. A person has treated someone else's property—*yours*--with no respect and pretended the 'false witness' command doesn't matter. How is that unclear? What happens the day people decide they have the 'right' to take things off your property—because they've 'evolved' or law has 'evolved' to that point, like the teenage boy in Chicago who says he's a girl and has the right to shower in the highschool girl's locker room?"

"It would never happen." Michael protected himself and his 'world.'

64

And left. But now he was bothered by that burning sensation in his wallet, burning like liquid oxygen, that hideous business card from Cam on which Cam had written his own number.

6

SEPARATIONS

"Excel-Land Excavating" Martin answered his phone, sounding unsettled these days by debt, rumors, a worried conscience and arguments with his woman when they did rarely cross paths on their opposite weekends. And drinking.

"Hello? Can I speak to Martin?" A deputy in Cam's office was calling from a cell phone.

"This is Martin."

"I got your number from a Michael Ostrand, that you clean up storm damage."

"Yeah, sure. What you got?"

"Yeah, it's a bit of a tangle of trees and muck. We've cut off what we could. I mean back at the beginning, we cut off what we had to to drive by on our road. But now we want to do the real thing. Get it straightened up. Could you come by tomorrow and see it?"

~ ~ ~

"Well, guess what I found, Shara?"

It was Elana, and her voice sounded alive.

"An old book by a person named Wallace in 1910 about 'new thoughts on Darwinism'. The thing is, I sort of skimmed all the scholarly stuff. It's also about how there is no point to anything in uniformitarianism. Life doesn't mean anything in that whole system. I don't know what happened to those people, but it's like they decided to stop asking *why* questions, and they just drowned themselves in their facts—or what they thought were facts, and even that wasn't done very well. The more I think about it, the more it's like the strangest step I've ever heard 'intelligent' people take.

"Oh, sure, we'll go solve a disease, or in Michael's case we'll figure out something about earthquakes and save tons of lives, or we'll protect some species. But that's not what I mean. I mean what the earth actually is. I mean that we are staying for a while on someone's property and you get these feelings once in a while that you know that this Person is a relative, but you've been too busy, or you heard a false account about what happened, and you've lost touch. But then you find out you really want to be in touch and it feels good to be close, and he does forgive, and he's the father you never... But some of us cut off our fathers..." She stopped.

"And?"

"I have been way outside what this 'Father's' world is actually about."

"Well, they—the universities, the media—have a lot of power. They are actually a mirror of the kind of power the Papacy and theocracies have had."

"True. But this stuff Cam works on, and some of those other speakers, it is powerful, too. It's compelling, but it's not imposed like uniformitarianism. It's just that someone wants it to fail. That's what I mean. The bottom. They don't talk about the bottom of all this, which is why they want Christianity to fail—or why they think that would be so good. They don't want anyone to know about what the world was really like back then or those other bizarre places and facts. Instead, *we're* the top of life, *we* are the ultimate goal, the intelligent ones."

"It's racism and other -isms. That is, it's all misunderstood. It's a cover-up for the racism intended by Huxley through his mule, Darwin."

"How do you mean?"

"Did you see AMAZING GRACE—the movie?"

"I sort of remember."

"That person—Wilberforce--was the bright spot ethically in the British scene at the time, right around 1800. He was as Christian as the converted slaver Newton, and he also wrote TRUE CHRISTIANITY, which the movie didn't mention. The movie didn't mention it because the subtitle of the book was about its contrast with the faith of the upper classes at the time. If the Left's intellectuals don't have upper class Christianity to blame for racism, then people might realize race superiority comes directly from evolution.

"Now, keep an eye on those upper classes. Because that's actually where the elite, racist scientists are going to come from. They are going to concoct something to battle the Christian movement, both its claim to truth and its impacts. The Empire was coming apart and other nations wanted independence, and the ruling classes of England were in a panic.

"Thomas Payne tried a direct attack on Christ. He just declared him to be totally nonsensical—teachings, miracles, everything. The problem was that Pastor Peter Holford circuited England in 1805 with his presentations on the historic truth of Christ in what he said about the destruction of Jerusalem 40 years ahead of time. It was proof about common, ordinary history. It wasn't just "in" the Bible. It answered quite a bit of Payne's attack, and Payne wasn't allowed to publish in England.

"Jefferson took the other response to Payne. He reduced Christ's sayings to those that were ethical. It was an answer to Payne of sorts, but did not have the impact that Holford did.

"So now the superior race and empire of England was at stake. That's why it was so difficult to get slavery stopped. It wouldn't have stopped by the usual procedures in the legislative houses; they had to do some clever diversions.

"So you have most of the Christians (like the large missionary movements that got going then) favoring an equality for the various nations and starting hospitals, etc., along with their preaching. But what do Huxley and Lyell do? They undercut all those Christian beliefs as 'impossible,' and the Creator as non-existent, so that the British race and empire can be supreme over them all. So that the 'endowing Creator' of the US Declaration of Independence is a myth, they said. It was war on the US Constitution.

"But they don't attack Christ. Huxley even promoted Sunday Schools for a while, but that's because they were the only education of most children took place at the time—children who worked 6 days a week. They attacked *Genesis* via their biology, which was dependent on geology because it needed billions of years. This was how the fractured world of knowledge has come down to us today. Fractured, split, fragmented. People like 'Christ' so long as it is not the Christ of the Bible—or as long as he has nothing to do with Genesis."

"Wow. Where did you get all that?"

"From listening to Cam's friends. I may sound like a professor, but I don't know a tenth of it. I just know that it is clear that racism doesn't come from Christianity; instead, *maintaining* racism was the goal of undercutting Christianity with evolutionary thought. The Left today should distance itself from uniformitarianism if it really wanted to stop racism, but it doesn't really, because racial strife will ruin the liberty provided by the Constitution. And guess who else took up that line, that *'struggle for superiority,'* once Christianity was 'dismissed' from 'intelligent discussion'?"

~ ~ ~

There was a knock on Jeff's door. It was Stacey. "What in the world?"

Stacy nodded humbly. "I know. It was stupid of me." She was very quiet.

"What happened?"

She looked away sideways. "Do we have to talk about it?"

"Well, yeah! But not now. Jump in the truck. Martin's got a new site he wants looked at. I need to be there in a few. Come on."

69

~ ~ ~

The customer appointment with Martin worked better than Cam thought because Jeff arrived as well by invitation from Martin. The plainclothes officer walked down the lane to meet them at a pile of debris. Police cars arrived behind them, blocking Martin and Jeff's vehicles. Cam stepped out of one.

Stacey was still explaining herself. "I just fell in love with California, and I mean it was effortless to meet friends... there... and... what's going on— I mean with the police here and all that? What are you working on?"

Cam had all the pieces he needed. "Martin Egland. You are under arrest for theft of personal property on or about the November 19th flood, and for obstruction of justice. You may remain silent, but everything you say can and will..."

Cam went on to repeat most of that for Jeff and Stacey. Additionally, Stacey's name had come up in lists of missing persons in California. "Stacey, we have an odd situation here. You're missing in California. But no one listed you *here*. Not even Jeff or your parents. Not a good situation for a girl to be in."

They were there for quite a while as Stacey's story was now another angle Cam had to consider in this tangle of debris and artwork and, now, humans.

~ ~ ~

Michael couldn't believe it was the same excavator he had hired. He sat in Cam's office, pleased at the discovery but embarrassed and angry about how much additional he had spent on a liar. "50% up front. So what happened to the carving according to these guys?"

"Remember the girl at the convenience store? It had drifted that far. To that driveway. Amanda was right to trust her suspicions. It was broken loose at high water—or high slurry--but obviously riding atop of the water and thus getting a mile or so that way and crossing which ever way the main channel went at that time. Finally there is a point where it gets stuck and enough mud and debris pile on top, and the force of the water at that point downstream has played out and can no longer move it.

"There are logarithms about things like this. The closer a floating object is to the most violent hydrology, the further it is found from it's start. The further the object is from that violent water, the closer to its start. A sort of a FILO pattern—first in, last out. I'd like to tell you about the Mayan solar calendar found in Queensland, Australia, in light of that, but it doesn't have anything to do with the carving."

70

"Oh, good grief, you and your 'Von Daniken' factoids! Then what?"

"Well, then a hard-luck criminal mind takes over. He's helping those 5 residents by opening their lane late that night when he sees it. He just does a minimum of work and covers it up so that he can return the next night in the dark. He's desperate for money and sees something that might clear him 5 grand if he does it right. Apparently he thought of checking the neighborhood to make sure its home wasn't right around the corner. Credit him with that.

"The next night in the dark, he came with Jeff and a rental van. The bright yellow sign that the Amanda's mother saw in the middle of the night was actually the side of the van showing occasionally in the front-end loader's lights. He used a sling and had Jeff drive it to their house, where Jeff got cleaning supplies and Stacey and took off for California. They rinsed it thoroughly at a truck stop south of Olympia, and we have a recording of that, but not the best view. By the time Jeff was north of Sacramento where you might turn off for the Bay area, Martin had his first response on eBay, targeting Lake Tahoe and BayArea property owners. They drove to Marinwood in the hills north of the Golden Gate, following a buyer."

"A buyer?"

"Just the new owner's landscape service is all. The foreman went over to a junction and checked it out, and approved the piece as something he could work into the whole landscape. Then it was delivered. The sling was still in place. The nicks and scars kind of made an endearing impression on the homeowner, like it had had a rough life. The broken antler point was just thought to be part of that. Jeff seems to have had no idea.

"A deputy sent me a silt sample from the belly area of the mane— thanks to the extra detail that Fisher carved into it. There was enough to go on, and nothing like soil in northern California, etc. It was an easy match. Then we tried sifting that soil at Amanda's driveway and they only went through three scoops before the antler tip showed up. It was clearly a match."

"How much did he get?"

"That was $6000."

"What happens now?"

"It's an unusual situation. It's all installed there in Marinwood. I think the owner would be perfectly happy to return it. You two can work that out. Fisher might get a nice piece of work replacing one for him. One thing we have to delve into further as far as planned criminal activity is just whether they put together this diversion in which Stacey disappeared."

"What's that about?"

"When everyone arrived at the staged customer stop this week, I noticed something strange about Stacey. She was genuinely surprised that the arrest was taking place. Her emotions were clear and that's a huge clue. If they had staged her disappearance, Stacey would have come across phony.

71

But she truly had no idea. I don't think they were smart enough to devise a cover diversion. She really did just wander off into town there, soaking in sunshine and 'enjoying paradise.' It is amazing that she showed up the very day, the hour, that Jeff was headed out the door. Or else it's suspicious."

"Like you said, that's the skillset of your job."

"You have to."

"Do you?"

"You *have* to, to really know what's going on in these things. So little of the world is the silent, sterile, event-free diorama of the anthropology museums, with dinosaurs chewing plants in the distance and cave-people pounding out grains. Michael, just think as a scientist about the odds of Stacey arriving back at Jeff's after 4 months at the very moment, he's going out the door to be trapped by us. What does that tell you?"

"I don't know. It sounds like something a novel writer would arrange for dramatic impact."

"So that what?"

"That's what I don't know—as far as the real persons go. Obviously the novel writer wants dramatic impact to sell novels!"

"Right. Well, we are ranging away from police business here. How about we get together and talk off the record, and maybe some more geology and the Grand Canyon. Or about God setting up events with unmistakeable timing. Like the size of the moon matching the sun during a solar eclipse."

"The Grand Canyon?"

"The logarithms? The Mayan calendar in Queensland?"

"Right, right. About the floating objects. Well, I still can't believe all this. This was a nice neighborhood; now it gives me the creeps. People who won't even ask around the area about a misplaced piece of valuable artwork that everyone knows. What if it was a Rembrandt?"

"And what about *Stacey*, Michael? She's more than a Rembrandt. She's a person they actually 'needed' to disappear for a mere 6 grand, or what little Jeff got out of it. Sheesh! How much are women worth these days, anyway? So now that some of the net gain and human capital of this is clear, do you see why God grieves about human sin, why he once decided to deluge almost all of it because of evil and violence?"

Michael was trapped on that one. His ears were very red.

~ ~ ~

That week, Elana was in the U District with Darcy to see a specialist. They would also try to stop in to see Michael at his office just before noon. But something triggered Elana's instincts and from a distance across the physical sciences concourse, she could see that Michael was in a bad mood. He was verbally lashing a geology student and shaming her in front of other students. Elana diverted Darcy and they moved away, but Elana tracked the girl as she walked to Elana's end of the concourse, and sat down, dejected. She turned out to be quite attractive, although she was obviously upset. Elana moved in for a conversation.

"You OK there?"

"I'll be OK."

"Anything innappropriate going on? I know all about 'reporting.'"

"'Reporting'? Oh...it's not that."

"But you're quite upset."

"Who are you?"

She sat beside her. "Well, I'm his partner. Ostrand's. For all intents and purposes, his wife. She's ours." She points to Darcy with her eyes. "But we're not on the best of terms right now."

"Oh. I'm sorry to hear that. Maybe God can heal it. You may be right. Maybe he was coming on to me...and that's why he was extra frustrated at what I believe."

"God?"

"Yeah. That's why I'm upset. Ostrand can't leave you alone. He can't leave your beliefs alone. There's Muslims in there and homosexuals and he never does this to them. I'm transferring out—I mean out of the program and I don't know what I'm going to work on now. I was having fun. Until I found out... You know, he's just a mirror fundamentalist. He has a 'Bible' and its Lyell's PRINCIPLES. I bet I won't get anywhere with a complaint to my advisor, either."

"I was watching from a distance. But I would say he shamed you."

"Yeah. Exempt."

"Exempt? I don't understand."

"The way all this is set up, my complaint would be exempt. I've read about it all over America's universities. It wouldn't matter what he did. He might even be able to hit on me, but because I think there was a global deluge like Genesis says, he can do what he wants here and nothing will happen for hitting on me...except praise from his peers."

Elana was furious. She now understood the end-game of the American university system as re-deployed after the uniformitarian invasion in the late 1800s. They'd sell everyone on rights here, rights there, rights for this girl to study geology, but wham!--if she said anything against their 'Bible.' They didn't really mean rights, after all. That was just icing that tricked you into eating their cake. "I'm Elana. Elana Morton."

"Marcona."

"We're in this together. Here's my number. Let me take care of Darcy, and then let's talk some more soon, OK? I just want you to meet another scientist before you decide about your career, I mean. He's a forensic scientist but he has a background in geology. He's a believer, too."

Marcona smiled and cried and wiped her eyes. "Wow. And you were just coming here...why?"

"Darcy. A specialist here at the U about something going on with her. But I'm a believer now, and it's because someone helped me see."

"Oh, I see. Thank you. Thank *God*. God brought you!"

Elana felt that inescapable tug.

"Mom! Come on!"

A young man approached to talk to Marcona. Elana smiled and nodded his way and left.

From a distance, Michael saw Marcona again, talking to a male classmate at the far end of the floor. Michael was still insensed as he glanced her way, shook his head and stepped back into an office.

~ ~ ~

Michael was taking in the mural of Monument Valley when Cam walked into the Great Southwest Restaurant where they met again for a coffee. Cam took note. They sat down.

"How have you been, Michael?"

"Err, something's strange about Elana. Distant. Like the folk lyrics, I guess. *'Where does it say 'Love lasts forever'?'*"

"Oh, I'm sorry to hear that. How does that make you feel?"

Michael was stumped at that one. "I've had enough of the violated feeling about the carving and those creeps. In fact, I don't even want to hear about whether they planned or staged the Stacey diversion."

"Yeah. 'Do not steal' sounds pretty real to you right now."

"Right."

"So that's why I just wondered how you felt, about Elana."

"I don't want to talk about it. Except something happened back when the carving went missing."

"Howdoyoumean?"

"I just don't think she cared anymore."

"Cared? About what?"

"Look, I don't know. I came here because you wanted to tell me something about the Grand Canyon or something. You think you have something about the geology of the river, about sediment or something and your video presentation."

It was looking like it would not be a good day to talk to Michael after all.

"What did Fisher think when he heard about what happened?"

74

"He keeps talking about that relative's spirit. The ancestor. Oh, who cares? They can just believe what they want."

"What does he believe?"

"That the ancestral spirit protected it on its odyssey. That the orcas knew that some Suquamish artifacts were on that ferry that day when they leaped out of the water as it approached Suquamish."

"You see, Michael, I know you find that superstitious, right? And all that is supposed to be nonsense, right? Like children not stepping on sidewalk cracks? Or like Muslims saying the world is balanced on the back of huge turtle, and that's what makes for earthquakes."

"Yeah."

"And out at the ocean, a tribe found a petroglyph that had been forgotten or misplaced for generations. It's a pictogram of Raven the Creator defeating a lizard."

"What's that got to do with anything?"

"They both conflict with uniformitarianism, don't they? They are saying there has to be a Creator and there has to be an account in which people are more than biological developments, that they are in contact with that Creator and what he says is right. You and Fisher agree that the theft of the carving was wrong, but there's something you don't share with Fisher, and that's a higher reason or basis for saying something wrong took place. Not that I think it stands on superstition in my case; but at least they don't believe law itself is evolving like Langdell at Harvard. They believe law is rooted in the Creator. Listen to the Suquamish legend: the Creator gave humans, animals and plants the ability to *form-change*. But they deceived each other. So He took the ability away. They have been in their set forms ever since."

"I do believe the theft was wrong! It was *my* property!"

"Yes, it was! Which is why Genesis and creation is appealed to when God in the Bible says do not steal, along with all the other basic commands. His image is that he creates things; *'the earth is the Lord's and all it contains.'* We are made in that image and have things we create too. We are violated when our things are stolen. God is violated when His things are taken."

Cam stopped and let it be absorbed. "Actually, there isn't any other command; they are all a form of theft."

"Huh? I thought you guys believed in 10?"

"We do, but look at them closely, and they all come down to theft of one kind or another." Cam stopped again and let Michael speak next.

After a few minutes Michael blurted out "Why do you keep asking me about Mount Saint Helens? It's an anomaly."

"Well, I'm just surprised that a Lyellian would say such a thing. He said 'we can only trust in processes we can see.' And yet when an event comes along captured in hours of footage and rooms full of measurements, you, as a leading university geologist, call it an anomaly instead of saying 'time to rewrite all we know about the subject.' So much for 'processes we can see.'

"What would there be to rewrite?"

"The explanation as to why so many feet of sediment in Grand Canyon are from New England, for starters. The speed with which the face of the earth can change."

"You said 'God' flooded the world because it was evil and violent, right?"

"That's right." Cam sensed a slow wheel moving.

"What would that look--" he didn't finish his question. "I can't talk about this right now." Michael got up to leave. He chipped in a ten.

Cam reflected and waited for a finale. But there was none. Michael left. Cam prayed for Michael, paid, and left.

~ ~ ~

It was quite late on one of his on-campus days when Michael came home. It was now April, but he could have sworn it was like January after Christmas— or what was left of Christmas in the Ostrand-Morton home. Or what was left of the Ostrand-Morton home.

That was exactly the point of that moment when he rolled in. He could feel it. There was no home. There was *no one* home. There was a letter on the kitchen table at home and it was set for dinner for one and the oven was on low.

Michael,
The kids and I are safe. I promise you with every resource I have they will be safe. We have left for a while. We don't know how long. We care about you and we know you care about us, but we don't want to go through the rejection we feel from you about the things we now believe about God. We don't know if God is ever going to change things for Darcy but that's not the point. We just don't want to be around while you are fighting with whatever it is they did to you as a student and which you do to other students like Cam and you actually did to Marcona. She and I talked.

If you could just realize the 'fact' or maybe it's the 'factor' that God is there and can do these things they are talking about and that He is to be honored, then we think the whole structure will change for you. But it's for you to wrestle, work through. Just think: the whole elk thing may have happened so you could see the utter sense of God's commands. But you have to see that on your own, not through your kids. And not me.

If you could just see that everything Cam and Shara have been saying reinforces a <u>marriage</u>, then I could talk to you. It makes perfect sense to us, *and there's several reasons for that. But I have no idea how long it will take you to get there, because you will go back to your Lyell and to his magnificent method, and that's what you want.*

But I want marriage, and I'm going toward the things that support that, and the One who created that. And that's what I want the kids to have the opportunity to see and know because they are innocent. I don't want animal-mating forced on them. I don't want un-marriage forced on them. Because as my knowledge of the truths in Christian teaching has risen, so has my need to have the values and virtues and traits that are in it.

You must understand this; I just can't see you not understanding this. But I guess you don't, and until I see that you do, I have to raise them unconflicted. They are children, and they shouldn't be raised in a war! 'A house divided will not stand.'

You have my number. You can see them any time. But I don't think you want to see them unless you can dominate them. Which I dread. But I will make arrangements for them to get to you, and ask that you honor their wishes through it all. They know why I'm doing this, and they know they are free to see you and are free to leave you. If you can't agree to that, don't bother calling.

I've copied this note and mailed it to my counselor and to a mediator. I'm sure you don't want a bunch of legal crap to deal with. I don't. And I'm not attached to anything or the place, except these beliefs and the kids and their futures. This is about the right, the freedom, in America to believe what you have reasons for, and what you think are reasons, not what some professional class says you have to believe and for their reasons.

Respectfully,

Elana

79

Combined Background Resources and Glossary
Marcus Sanford, ask@interplans.net

Ager, D. THE NATURE OF THE STRATIGRAPHICAL PROCESS. A peer scientist disputes Lyell's basis for uniformitarianism by evidence about rapid deposition and the Epeiric sea over north America.

Ager, D. NEW CATASTROPHISM.

Armour, R. North American Indian Fairy Tales, Folklore and Legends, (1905). Ojibwe legend of Nanabohzo.

Appearance of Design. The recognition even by Dawkins that the earth and its occupants seem to be here and formed to be here by design.

Baugh, C. PRE-FLOOD ARTIFACT DEVASTATES UNIFORMITARIANISM. Youtube. A hammer made of sophisticated metal from England in a 'strata' where it does not 'belong.'

Baugh, C. THE WORLD AND MANKIND BEFORE THE FLOOD. Youtube. "Bizz-artifacts" of the ancient world re longevity, giantism.

Baumgardner, J. CATASTROPHIC PLATE TECTONICS; the key to understanding the Genesis Flood. Youtube.

"Biblical-Type Floods Are Real, and They're Absolutely Enormous" DiscoverMagazine.com. 2012-08-29.

Boudreaux. NEW THEORY FOR THE PRE-FLOOD CANOPY re sugilite, a trace mineral found all over the earth's surface. Youtube.

Bretz, J H. 1920s. Geologic catastrophism in connection with Lake Missoula.

Brown, W. (various titles on the deluge and anomalies left around the world by it, but usually written apart from tectonic theory). Former DOD logistician.

Carbera, Dr. A Peruvian surgeon who located a human skull in tertiary material with dinosaurs.

CENTRALIA THEORY. A newer catastrophic view that the entire central 80% of Australia is a rapid deposit sedimentary zone as part of a global event.

Chima Channels, Peru. Advanced water supply systems that moved water 150 miles in 'primitive' times.

Clark, E. INDIAN LEGENDS OF THE PACIFIC NORTHWEST. One of the best collections. The great flood is a frequent subject.

Clemens, J. Research on granitic magmatism. Geologist Association of London.

Coconino. The layer of sandstone at Grand Canyon that is from northeast north America.

Cooper, B. AFTER THE FLOOD.

CREATION. A recent production about the domestic and social factors that mattered while Darwin wrote ORIGINS.

Creationwiki.com. 8700 articles.

Crone, B. IN THE DAYS OF NOAH. Giants, Ancient Technology and Noah's Ark. Part 2: A Glorious Civilization. A very complete collection of archeological and geological anomalies, however, some examples did not have to do with the Genesis flood as such, simply other artefact anomalies.

DARWIN'S DILEMMA. Illustra Media. Even with a major flaw in the system, Darwin proceeded—or could not stop Huxley from pushing it out to the public now that the theory had "geological" support from Lyell and Hutton.

Dona, K. ARTEFACTS FROM PRE-FLOOD WORLD & FALLEN ANGELS. Pres. By Habsburg Haus curator. Youtube. "Bizz-artefacts" of the ancient world.

Epeiric Sea. The worldwide ancient sea as referred to in scientific literature, to which Pangaea (one single continent) was the counterpart.

Farellian Law of Chance. 1:1 (50th) is the point of impossibility. Most of the critical doctrines of evolution and uniformitarianism are dependent on much less favorable odds.

FINDING NOAH. Oct.8.2015 limited screening documentary.

Geo-mythology. The science of connecting ancient myth to its location's fossils or artefacts.

Giem, P. IS PLUTO YOUNG? Youtube.

GILGAMESH EPIC. Babylonian flood account as part of a search for eternal life after offending a female deity. Only Utnapushtim has eternal life; he responded to deity instructions to build a huge ship, titled The Preserver of Life, and survive a flood that would otherwise destroy all life. He took his family, village craftsmen, and baby animals.

Guthrie. FROZEN FAUNA... Research on the plant life around the time and place of the huge numbers of frozen mammoths.

Hancock, G. FINGERPRINTS OF THE GODS. Former ECONOMIST correspondent compiles all the archeological and geological anomalies which orthodox science simply won't mention in public.

Haynes. MAMMOTHS... Research on the thousands of mammoths in permafrost.

Hovind, K. FLOOD OF NOAH. Youtube. Hundreds of flood legends around the world. Hovind tends to wander off topic.

Hovind, K. THOUSANDS OF DRAGON LEGENDS AROUND THE WORLD. Youtube. Hovind tends to wander off topic.

Howorth, 1887. Early research on mammoths unable to explain the huge numbers found in permafrost.

Hippolytus. Ancient Greek historian who described worldwide flood as consisting of water from below, and fire and earthquakes.

James-Griffiths, P. TRACING GENESIS THROUGH ANCIENT CULTURE. Youtube. Extensive and well-illustrated comparative legend and literature. Two British antiquities curators explain why Genesis is the literary source of the numerous world accounts of cataclysms.

Jenkins Collection. A huge collection of Naszca materials that was extremely difficult to access for many years. See Naval Observatory of Peru.

Job 9. 'God moves and overturns mountains.'

Johnson, C. THE PRE-FLOOD WORLD: CREATION AND CANOPY. Youtube.

Langdell. Doctor of Law appointed at Harvard in 1879 primarily because he used ORIGIN OF SPECIES concepts and language to reshape American law.

LIVING WATERS. See nrbtv (Direct 378). This is a rich photoessay against several aspects of Darwinism.

Lewis, C. S. GOD IN THE DOCK. Among these essays, besides the one featured here, "The Myth That Became Fact" is a complete statement as to why we should expect near-replica accounts from all the ancient cultures that are 'memories' of what actually happened. Simply for the reason that it actually happened!

Lyell. Mid-1800s scientist who developed the idea of uniformitarianism 'to free geology from Moses.'

THE MAN WHO FOUND TIME. Re Hutton (mid-1700s) and the first attempts to state the view that there are vast amounts of time manifested on earth.

Mayr, E. THE NATURE OF THE DARWINIAN REVOLUTION.

Mayor, A. Folklorist and geomythologist. Her hypothesis was that seashells and marine fossils found inland and on mountains inspired worldwide flood legends.

Mial, A. (research on failures of uniformitariansm) Springer International Publishing.

Naval Observatory of Peru. One of the current locations of the former Jenkins collections of Nazsca stones and artefacts, along with the Aeronautical Museum of Peru.

National Geographic Society. (100 mammoths at Hot Springs, South Dakota).

Noa A Gomshi. Translation: Noah's Huge Boat. The local name for the Ararat area.

Noorberger, R. SECRETS OF THE LOST RACES. Peruvian and other evidence shows a very different world before a global deluge.

NOVA. Making North America. Nov. 2015. The usual uniformitarianism but only about north America and its dinosaurs. Metal particles sprayed around when an asteroid struck. "Every layer we see used to be the surface of the earth" in perfectly predictable order (!).

Nurre, P. EGYPTIAN CHRONOLOGY AND THE BIBLE. Nwcreation.net. Comparing new archeology with Biblical record.

Oard, M. THE LAKE MISSOULA FLOOD. Nwcreation.net Seattle creation conference 2015. This event echos the Genesis flood and demonstrates what happens when a half-continent floods.

Oard, M. WHAT HAPPENED TO WOOLLY MAMMOTHS? Nwcreation.net Seattle creation conference 2015. Newest research on the thousands of mammoths frozen upright in permafrost, 'drowning' in *loess*.

Ocucaje village. Peruvian village where many of the sketched burial stones were found. Samples of methods of preserving human flesh. Excavated in 1950 by Solde. Patination confirmed by the University of Bonn.

Opisthotonic. The feature of many fossils which appear to have been pressed, flattened, or smashed by abrupt overwhelming force against a rock surface.

Physico-theologians. Those pastors and professors in the 1800s who believed God originated and sustained each organism on a micro level, but not in a pantheistic sense. *'In all life Thou livest / the true life of all.'* Sometimes the view *sounded* quaint, but it was sheer skepticism and a desire for another outcome, not facts, that ridiculed it.

Pluto's mountains. A critical dating item which has lead in part to removing Pluto from the planet list because they are 'too young.'

Prescott, W. THE CONQUEST OF PERU. Early data on advanced civilization and young creation.

Psalm 104. The creation psalm with a few verses on the deluge, if not on Gen 1:2.

Psalm 136. The earth is set on top of water.

SATAPATHA BRAHMANA. The Hindu version of the great flood. The 1st man Manu is warned of impending flood and advised to build a giant boat.

Schaeffer, F. GENESIS IN SPACE AND TIME. A bit dated on some information, but mentioned the extensive accounts of massive flooding among South American peoples.

Siccar Point, Scotland. This site is contested as a clinching site by both uniformitarians and Biblical creation/deluge believers.

Silvestru, E. GEOLOGY AND DEEP TIME. Youtube. Vertical tectonics, rapid sedimentary deposits by a highly-trained ex-uniformitarian.

SHA NAQBA IMURU. Ancient Bablylonian text containing GILGAMESH EPIC. The title means "He who saw the deep." (Deep = the unfathomable waters, oceans).

Snelling, A. WORLDWIDE FLOOD; GEOLOGIC EVIDENCE. Youtube. Demonstrates some calculations of how hundreds of feet of sediment could have been transferred 2000 miles.

Steno, N. Mid-1600s 'father of geology' and his Biblical basis.

Stratigraphy. The 'account' of earth history in the layers or strata of geology.

Superfault. A location where the mantle is known to have buckled between 100-10,000 meters in one moment.

Tihuanaca, Peru. Gateway to the Sun construction; metal staples to connect massive stones; temples similar to those in Cambodia; earthquake protection that has worked; universal ethnicity in the facial carvings; jade used in carvings is from China.

Timeaus. Plato's account of a flood over the whole earth. A Titan named Prometheus tells Deucalion it is coming, who prepares and survives it.

Titikaka., Peru. Native boats memorialize sea-monster accounts.

Tolmachoff. 1929. Studies on woolly mammoths as anomalies.

Vereshagin. MAMMOTH CEMETERIES. Research on cause of death of thousands of mammoths in permafrost.

Uniformitarianism. The view that there has been no creation of or interaction by a deity (god) with our universe. It is entirely a matter of ordinary scientific laws and events.

Walker, T. (THE GENESIS DELUGE). Nwcreation.net Seattle creation conference 2015. Worldwide samples of tectonic upheaval and sedimentary transfer.

Walker, T. MEGA-CATASTROPHE. Nwcreation.net Seattle creation conference 2015.

Wallace, A. NEW THOUGHTS ON EVOLUTION. 1910 critique of where it was headed. Material on Haeckl.

Waltke, B. CREATION AND CHAOS. Study of ancient near east legend to show how Genesis 1's mission is to declare that the LORD is the redemptive-creator.

Ward. CALL OF THE DISTANT MOUNTAINS. Research on the anomalies of woolly mammoths.

Wikipedia. Final introductory quote about Genesis flood: *"A world-wide deluge, such as described in Genesis, is incompatible with modern understanding of the* natural history *and especially* geology *and* paleontology." (!)

Wilberforce, W. English politician and evangelical Christian who helped end slavery in England in the early 1800s and wrote a criticism of upper class life and Christianity for its attempt to preserve slavery.   To preserve race superiority, evolutionary doctrines were accepted, on both sides of the Channel.

Woodman. NASZCA; JOURNEY TO THE SEA. The scope of their balloon technology was similar to Kon Tiki and the sea.

Ziusudra Epic. Sumerian. The preflood kings lived enormous life spans. After the flood their lifespan is normal.

Interplans.net story development can take an idea from a single line to placing it as a motion-picture script in an archive for producers to browse.

Notes

Notes

Notes

71119050R00050

Made in the USA
Columbia, SC
21 May 2017